Winter Is My Middle Name

By

DW Rayner

Dedicated to my wife Darlene, my daughters Heather & Erin, my grandchildren Collin, Ethan & Jaxon, and my son-in-law John. Thank You All!

January nips the fingers and bites the toe
February is full of ice and snow
March winds down the chimney blow
April showers
Bring May flowers
June pretty flowers everywhere
Warm July our nation's birthday
August ripens peach and pear
School begins in warm September
In October leaves all fall
Turkeys come in bleak November
Then comes December, best of all!

My mother knew that old poem by heart and would always say it in the winter. I think deep down she really liked winter almost as much as I did. Now, many years after she has gone, my wife and I are taking down our Christmas tree on January 2. This has become a tradition and it is still just as sad now as when I was a kid. Even though I hate putting the tree up in December, come January, I hate to take it down. I don't know if this will be our last Christmas together when you get old you start thinking about things like this and your past in general.

As I look out the window there is no snow in sight. This has been the warmest winter I can recall since the early 1960s. That was a year like this and I thought it would never snow, but snow it did! I was ready to run away to Canada, there is always snow there I thought. That was my goal in life, to go to Canada and build a log cabin along a desolate lake. Just fish, trap animals, cut firewood, and have a small vegetable garden with fruit trees all around. Yes, I had it all planned out I could not wait to get out of school. It was a waste of time I knew how to read, write, and do arithmetic, that was all I needed to know, or so I thought at the time. Enjoy this look back at a simpler time, when no one locked their doors and kids could play outside and roam the neighborhoods without fear of anything happening to them. I can hear my mother telling me, "Just be home when the streetlights come on." There were pay phones everywhere, cell phones weren't invented, and not everyone had a television. It was a fun time growing up in Johnstown, Pennsylvania, and we enjoyed every minute. I hope you enjoy reading this book as much as I enjoyed writing it.

Table of Contents:

Chapter 1

There I was, trudging home from school. Normally I would be running home; the sooner I got away from the school the better. Christmas vacation was too short; they should give us the three winter months off from school and let us go to school in the summer. It was January 2; this was always the saddest day of the year. Not only did I have to go back to school, but it would also mean that when I got home, my mother would be taking down the Christmas tree! I hated to see the Christmas season come to an end. I loved Christmas and anything that involved snow or ice. "Winter" was my middle name! I could not stand being in the house. It didn't matter how cold it was outside, I would spend every minute I could sled riding, skiing, or just walking in the snow. I loved it! When I came into the house, my fingers would start to sting and I would run cold water over them to take the pain away.

We had snow at Christmas, but now there were only traces of it where the snowplows piled it up along the streets or where it was heaped up along the sidewalks after being shoveled. The piled up snow was turning black from the soot and coal smoke spewing out of the chimneys on houses and from the smokestacks at the mill. At the other end of town, the snow piles were turning a rusty brown color from the open hearths and the blast furnaces. We lived in the west end of town and the wind blew everything toward the east end.

At least my father would not be at home with his yelling "Fiddlesticks!" at everything he didn't agree with. He was working 3-11 in the steel mill and I would be in bed long before he got home. He was from England and believed in the class system, and of course he was at the top. He thought everyone was put on earth to serve him and "children should be seen, and not heard."

During World War II, he was a radioman in the British Navy; he always called it the "Royal Navy." He had a way of using words like "lorry, flat, loo, fag, blimey, and cheerio." My friends had no idea what he was talking about, and for the longest time I thought "little bugger" was a term of endearment. When I would bring a friend home, he would ask me, "What's that little bugger up to?" It wasn't until I was grownup that I found out that it had a very different meaning.

When he was home my mother had to cook meat, potatoes, gravy, and vegetables for every meal; I hated all these big meals. I only "ate to live," I didn't "live to eat" like my pal Tubby, he would eat constantly! Now mom could open a can of soup, or make hamburgers or hotdogs, and we both would be happy.

My father had been stationed in Baltimore for a month while they made repairs to his ship and my mother had been working there at the Social Security office as a keypunch operator. It was New Year's Eve and they met in a dark, smoke-filled little bar. Three weeks later they were married. That is how my mother was, very impulsive, I think everyone who knew her must of thought she had lost her mind. A week later, he shipped out and occasionally she would receive a letter from him. It was during the war and they could only send mail when they went into a port. The letters would be postmarked "Cape Town," "Sierra Leone," or some other exotic place. The remainder of the time were out looking for Nazi warships. After the war was over, my father returned to England and sent for my mother. They lived there for several years and that is where I was born during the "storm of the century." I imagine that was why I enjoyed winter so much.

My mother did not like living in England; she said it was too wet and cold. It was a custom in England to put the babies outside for at least twenty minutes everyday. They believed it was very healthy for them; perhaps they were right.

My mother would go shopping and leave me outside in the pram with all the other babies. One day she came out and there was a horse looking into the pram and she almost had a heart attack. That was when she finally convinced my father to come back to Johnstown. He found a job in the steel mill and they rented a house in "Ducky Beach." There were no ducks and no beach, just a great view of the Conemaugh Gap and the steel mills. This section of town did not have sewers, so we had an outhouse, cold running water, and electricity. We eventually got a telephone.

I remember my mother heating water on the stove so I could take a bath. There was a big, maroon enamel Kalamazoo coal stove in the middle of the kitchen to heat the house. We used to sit at the kitchen table in front of the stove and listen to "Superman" and "Fiber Magee and Molly" on the radio. The public sidewalk went right by our window and we would see women coming home from shopping, carrying their bags, or coal miners with their lunch buckets, stooped over from a hard day's work, covered with coal dust, coming home.

My father could not believe there was not a toilet in the house. He said he was going to get a "real" house even if he had to build it himself, and eventually he did. That is how we came to be living in a cement block foundation. It was like living in a cave. Most of it was below ground except for the back where the door was located. The few windows we had were high up and you could not see anything out of them, except for the sky.

I was walking past Silver's Drug store and I stopped to look into the big glass window. It didn't matter what the weather was like, the glass was always clean. There was a long counter with old-fashioned stools with backs on them, not like the more modern round stools at the Dairy Dell. The floor was made up of small black and white octagon tiles, and when I had money to spend, I would go inside for the best milkshake five cents could buy. Then I remembered we had to take the tree down and I knew I should get moving and get it over with. There would be no changing my mother's mind and I might as well not even try. Up ahead I saw my pal Tubby; he wasn't what you would call fat, just big. I ran up to him and tapped him on the back. He jumped a foot off the ground, which was high for his size!

"What're you trying to do Danny? Scare the crap out of me!"

"Take it easy Tubby, that would take a lot a scaring. I have to get home to help take down the Christmas tree."

"Taking it down already? Aren't you going to leave it up for the Russian Christmas?"

"Naw, my Dad wouldn't want anyone to think we were Russians!" The Russian Christmas was celebrated on January 7, and from our neighborhood we could look across the valley over to the Russian neighborhood where it looked like every house was lit up.

My dad would put a ten-watt candle in the window and that was our outside decoration. Although one year after Christmas he found two sets of outdoor lights, with eight bulbs on each string, on sale for ninety percent off, and he bought them. That was all he talked about for a week. How he got those lights for only ten percent of the

3

original price. He thought it was the deal of the century! The following year he put them on the two small evergreens on each side of our front door. Well, eight lights on those trees did not cover much. It was the skimpiest looking outside decoration I ever saw. I think we were the talk of the neighborhood that year. He never put them up again.

"Hey, are you going skating Friday at Faiths Grove?" I asked Tubby.

"It's Friday, isn't it? Of course I'll be there." Tubby also lived to roller skate; he was there everyday they had skating. He would also go over to Roseland, Skateland, or Skate Away and skate there if he had enough money.

"I'll see you there, since we haven't had much snow yet this winter. I would sooner be sled riding or skiing in the graveyard." The graveyard was like our private park; it was where we played football, baseball, and went skiing and sled riding.

"I'm going with Joe. We'll meet you at the graveyard at 6:30, OK?"

"Ok, I'll be there. You know, I really don't like Joe. He's always getting me into some kind of trouble."

"You don't like anyone, you know that? It's not just you; he gets everyone into trouble!"

He was right. I didn't have any "best" friends; Tubby was about as close to a best friend as I would ever get. We had a lot in common. He was an only child like me, and our fathers worked shifts in the mill. I guess I was sort of a loner. I didn't mind being by myself. It seemed in those days that when you were with your "friends" it involved a lot of hitting each other, which I didn't like. If you were walking down the street with your "buddy," and he spied an empty Lucky Strike cigarette pack on the sidewalk, he would jump on it while at the same time punching you in the arm yelling "Lucky Strike!!" Or if he found an empty Camel cigarette pack, he would pick it up and ask "Hits or cracks?" You would respond with either and it seemed like no matter which one you said you would end up getting punched in the arm. He would peel off the blue tax stamp to reveal either an "H" or a "C" and would say either "You're right, its "H'" and punch you or if it was a "C" you would get punched because you were wrong. When someone punched me I

4

would go crazy, I could not explain it. So that is probably one reason I didn't have many close friends.

I just tried to get along with everyone I was with at the moment, but there was something about Joe I just didn't like. He had a way of getting into trouble without even trying. If you were sitting next to him on the playground, in the next moment you would be running for your life because some big kid was running after Joe and anyone he was with, yelling, "I'll kill you!" I never knew what he did to those guys to make them so angry, but they sure didn't like him.

"Yeah, yeah, I'll see you there!"

When I arrived home, my mother, who was as tough as nails, had all the ornaments off the tree and put in the boxes. She was now taking off the icicles and saving them for next year. I could never understand why she didn't just throw them out with the tree; they were only ten cents a box! I guess it had something to do with growing up during the "Great Depression" that I always heard about. She was always telling me how lucky I was to have all the things that I had. When she was little she had to make her own clothes out of gunnysacks, and they itched!

She always had that Lucky Strike cigarette hanging out of her mouth. When they coined the phrase "chain smoker" they must have had her in mind. As she talked, the cigarette would bounce up and down between her lips like a twig bouncing in the wind. It was amazing to watch. I don't know how she did it, but the ash never did fall off. She had an ashtray on every table and would flick her ash into the closest one as she went about her daily routine.

My father, on the other hand, was a Camel smoker. A little too strong for my taste, I preferred the "Luckies." He would also smoke a pipe or cigars, whatever was closest. The steelworkers smoked cigarettes (or "fags" as my father called them), coalminers used snuff (either Copenhagen or Skoal) and the refractory workers used side chew (like Mail Pouch or Beechnut). And they all liked their beer!

My father was a "jack of all trades, master of one." He was an expert in electrical, radio, and television repair. When our 1933 Plymouth would break down, I would hear him yelling, "Fiddlesticks, that damn throw out bearing went again!" Although this was not electrical, he became an expert. He would replace throw out bearings as often as other people changed oil. He could change that bearing in two hours. He would be out in the street in front of our house and would be lying under the car with just his feet sticking out. His feet would turn one way then another, and then disappear all together. I would have to stay there the whole time just in case he needed something. Every now and then you would hear "Oh fiddlesticks!" and some mumbling. I would pretend I didn't hear anything.

My parents called that old car the "Green Hornet." They gave all of our cars names. I didn't know of anyone else that did this and I never told my friends about it. Our next "new" car was a 1950 Studebaker, the model that had the rocket-shaped front end; they called it "True Blue Trudy." It was blue, just like the Plymouth was green. We never bought a brand new car; any car with less than 50,000 miles was new to my father. I am not sure if he realized that the odometer only went to 99,999 miles, and then went back to 0. I am sure all the cars he bought had over 100,000 miles on them. They all had some sort of defect.

"I ran into Tubby on the way home and we're going skating on Friday," I told my mother.

"What else is new? You go skating every Friday. You don't know how lucky you are that you can do that. During the "depression" we could only afford food, and we were very grateful for it, not like some people I know." Then of course she was looking right at me. My father would get so upset that I didn't eat everything on my plate. I just wasn't a big eater, He would have liked the way Tubby could eat! Then my mother would try to defend me and he would say "Fiddlesticks," and that would be the end of the discussion.

"Who all is going skating?"

"Me, Tubby, and Joe."

"I don't like that Joe kid. Ever since his father died, he seems to have gone off the deep end. And Tubby, well you know what his mother did don't you? She went and painted all her kitchen appliances BLACK! Can you believe that? They'll be locking her up in the loony bin soon! White is the only color they come in, just go look in Sears or Montgomery Ward. Did you ever see a green fridge or stove? NO, and no yellow or pink and especially not BLACK! I just couldn't believe it when I heard about it. So you better watch that Tubby kid, it just may be hereditary!"

6

With that she left the room shaking her head and mumbling to herself. She was the school truant officer and that was how she knew so much about everyone. Then she stopped and turned around and said, "I just remembered, we have to go up to Farmer Black's place. He didn't send his kids to school again and he can't blame the weather; we haven't had much snow yet and hunting season is over. I don't know what is going on up there."

It was always an eerie drive up there to that farm. The trees above the steep road bank had roots sticking out of them like arms with hands and long gnarled fingers that dug deep into the ground to keep them from falling over on to the dirt road below. The sign at his property line stated: "KEP OWT." I am not the best speller, but even I knew "KEEP" had two "E's.

"Oh man! I don't want to go up there! Remember what happened to us the last time? That darn pig chased you down the road! I think he left him out on purpose. Can't you wait until dad can take you?"

That pig was as big as a Nash Metropolitan! My father and I waited out in the car with the motor running. He was sitting in the driver's seat of our 1933 Plymouth, looking over his shoulder, watching the old farmhouse. He saw what was happening and he leaned over and opened the passenger door just as my mother reached the car. She jumped in and slammed the door shut just as the pig got to the car. It was a close one. My father floored the gas pedal and we took off at breakneck speed, at least for a 1933 Plymouth, down that old Country Road. That episode would be remembered for years to come.

"I guess we could go up tomorrow before he goes to work. We'll see. I did want to get this tree out of the house before he comes home tonight."

"Sounds like a plan to me. I'll help you take it out. It's going to get dark soon anyway, and you don't want to go up the Country Road in the dark."

Friday finally arrived; for me it was the best day of the week during the school year. It meant no school for two days! Yippee! But then Sunday would come and I would keep thinking "I have to go to school tomorrow," and that ruined the whole day. I think Sunday was the worst day of the week.

I ran home from school and mom had made pancakes for supper. Now this was a meal I could get used to, but my dad would never hear of it. He would say, "Pancakes for supper? Fiddlesticks!" After we ate I ran to my room to get my dungarees and white tee shirt. When I opened the drawer, it was EMPTY! I couldn't believe it. Where were my clothes? What had happened?

"MOM, where are my clothes?"

"Because of the holiday I am a day behind on everything. I won't be washing clothes until tomorrow."

"Tomorrow? What am I going to wear to go skating tonight?"

"You can wear your dress clothes."

My dress clothes? She must have been kidding; I couldn't go skating in them! I would never live it down. Every kid there would be wearing the uniform of the era: dungarees, white tee shirt, clodhoppers, and a crew cut or a flattop hair cut. NOT dress clothes! It was bad enough that I was not allowed to wear clodhoppers, but there was NO way I was going there in dress clothes.

I looked in all my drawers, closet, laundry bag – NOTHING. I was doomed. I had to go skating; there was no snow to go sled riding or skiing - what else could I do on a Friday night? I put on my dress shirt, dress pants, and black shoes. Maybe no one would notice; it was winter and I had to wear a coat. But, I couldn't skate with a coat on. I was definitely doomed!

As I approached the graveyard, I could see Tubby and Joe sitting on a headstone waiting for me. I never would step on a grave let alone sit on a headstone; I knew better than that.

"Get off that stone," I yelled.

"The guy under here don't care what we're doing up here," replied Joe sarcastically. Oh, I didn't like that Joe!

"You got to learn to take it easy, Danny," yelled Tubby. "Hey! Look at YOU! Aren't you a DANDY!"

"What are talking about?" I pretended I had no idea what he meant.

"You're a DANDY in those dress duds."

"Hey! Don't say things like that!"

"Hey Danny is a Dandy, Danny is a Dandy," said Joe in a singsong voice.

Tubby yelled, "Lets go Dandy, we're going to be late."

"Hey you guys, cut it out. My dungarees are all in the wash. Tomorrow I will be wearing them again."

"Naw, I don't think so. I bet you're a Dandy now," yelled Joe.

"Shut up Joe! Quit calling me that."

"You going to make me?"

"Don't push me or I just might."

"Ha, ha, ha," he laughed as he shoved me away.

Just then Tubby stepped in and separated us. He knew what my temper was like. He found out the hard way. We were playing with his Marx - Fort Apache set, the one with the trading post, in his living room one day. I liked this set because it had the trading post. That would be where I would have to go for all of my supplies when I moved to Canada. I would trade the furs from the animals that I would trap for sugar, flour, coffee, and anything else that I would need. Yes, I had it all planned out.

I had the Indians and Tubby had the Cowboys. He punched me in the arm as he shot one of my Indians and yelled "I gotcha!" He did this a few times.

My immediate reaction was to hit him back, but I controlled myself. Then he hit me again, only harder, and I went berserk and was on top of him pounding him with all my might. His mother heard us and came running into the room and pulled me off of him while yelling "STOP IT!! You're going to kill him. Get off him right NOW!"

I didn't know what came over me. Tubby was twice my size and I am not a fighter, but when someone hits me, I just go crazy.

"Come on, let's go. I don't want to be late," Tubby hollered

Nothing more was said until after we got inside and started skating. Then Joe said "Hey Dandy, come and get me," as he skated away.

Then Tubby started doing the same thing and everyone was looking to see who Dandy was. I could hear someone saying, "That's not Dandy, its Danny" and "So is he Dandy now?" Then, after an hour or so, everyone in the entire rink was calling me "Dandy." I couldn't take it any longer, and I snuck out and went home early.

That was how I got my nickname "Dandy." Boy, I hated that the first few weeks. Everyone I saw was calling me Dandy. I couldn't believe how fast something like that got around the neighborhood and the school. I would run all the way home, through back alleys and side streets trying to avoid everyone, but I would always run into someone and they would say, "Hey Dandy, where you going?"

After a few weeks I figured it was no use fighting it, it was not going to go away. I may as well get used to being "Dandy." Maybe if everyone saw that it didn't bother me, they would quit calling me Dandy and I could go back to just being "Danny." No such luck. I would be known as Dandy for the rest of my life.

Things started looking up and I wore the nickname "Dandy" with pride. Even my mother and relatives started calling me Dandy - everyone except my father. He would only call me Dan or Daniel, not Danny and certainly not "Dandy."

It was a cold morning and I was eating my Puffed Rice; not because I liked it, but I wanted the land deed that was advertised on the box. The cereal's radio show was about Sergeant Preston, a Mountie in the Yukon. In each box of Puffed Rice and Puffed Wheat they would give away a deed to a square inch of land in the Yukon where Sergeant Preston and his trusty sled dog King had their adventures every week. After that, we cereal eaters were offered a one-ounce "poke" of genuine "Yukon dirt" for 25 cents. This was my goal in life, to move to Canada and get a dog sled and live by a lake in a log cabin. Like I said, I loved winter.

My mother came into the kitchen after going out for the newspaper and said, "The Russians are going to have a white Christmas. It smells like snow."

She could smell anything. I don't know how, being a chain smoker, but she could. I couldn't smell anything different from the day before, but she was usually right. About an hour later it did start to snow, and snow, and snow. I didn't think it would ever quit. It was twenty below zero and the winds were howling down from the mountaintops. Roads were drifted shut, vehicles were left abandoned in the middle of the streets; school was closed for the first time that I can remember. Life was Great! I would not have to run away to Canada after all.

We were lucky that we lived close to a dump. Other kids had to go to the hardware store for things; we just went to the dump and found everything for free. We were poor, but we never knew it. Tubby said he saw a Westinghouse refrigerator at the dump. Now this was the Cadillac of all refrigerators and had the best door for sledding. It had an Art Deco look with four rounded corners, not like the more modern boxy refrigerators with the square corners. The square corners would dig into the snow and the "sled" would not go anywhere. We knew this because we tried one last year and it was very disappointing.

All we had to do was to take off the handle and tie a rope through the hole and that Westinghouse door would fly down the hill at 30 miles an hour. Nothing would stop it! You could fit eight kids on it and all that weight made it go that much faster. This was going to be the best winter ever!

As I look back now, I often wonder how none of us were seriously injured. We would sled ride out into the street without looking for cars. Surprisingly none ever came. We would also climb to the top of the street, which was on a big hill. We would get a running start....fly down that street straight down the road through several intersections. No cars ever came in all the years we did this. I know there was not as much traffic then as there is now, but it is a wonder that a car never came. We were very fortunate.

We ran over to the dump before someone beat us to it. Luckily the fridge was still there, standing alongside a Wedgewood stove, both upright like two mighty sentries with old tires, rims, broken glass and other garbage lying all around. The door still intact. Tubby brought a hammer and a ten-penny nail to knock the pins out of the hinges. The handle was the only problem; it had to come off. It looked like a gearshift from a 1932 Ford pickup truck, with a round base and it protruded from the door at an angle. To open the door, you would pull on the handle and turn to the left or right.

Tubby had learned over the years how to get these off. He had made a mistake one year and he didn't take the hinges off first and after he took the handle off, the door would not open. We had to leave that refrigerator at the dump, sealed closed, never to be opened again. Sometimes you would see Tubby down there looking at that old thing; it was like he was paying his last respects to it. It was still there at the bottom of the dump and was now half buried with trash. In a year or two it would be completely covered.

Tubby looked at his Hopalong Cassidy wristwatch before he started. He was always trying to see if he could break his old record time of five and half minutes. He looked like a safe cracker that you see in the movies. He would cock his head to the side, put his ear near the base of the handle, and listen to the clicks as he gently swung the handle back and forth while at the same time pulling outward on it. He almost had it, I could tell by the big grin on his moon-like face.

But just then, it turned into a frown; something had gone wrong. The handle would not come off. Even though it was only twenty degrees outside, he was starting to sweat. He would move the handle to the left, then to the right, slowly, then faster. This went on for several minutes. There was no way he was going to break his record this year. I thought this fridge was going to end up with the other one at the bottom of the dump. Just then he swung the handle almost halfway around gave it a yank and it popped out and the smile returned to his face.

Now we had to pull it over to the graveyard; these things weighed a ton! I had brought an old piece of rope with me and we tied it onto the door and in no time flat we were on our way to try it out. The next problem was that all this snow was too fresh and deep to sled ride on. We went home and got our skis. Now these, of course, are not store bought skis. They were made from barrel staves that we found at the dump. We would find the widest stave, cut it in half and make a pointed tip where it was cut. Then an old belt was cut and nailed onto the staves for a strap for our feet. We would find an old candle and rub it on the bottom of the stave and we were ready to ski! After a few runs down the slope, the snow started to get packed down. More kids showed up with sleds, snow saucers, and coal shovels.

For those of you who are unfamiliar with shovel riding and have never slid down a hill on coal shovel, let me explain so you can try it out. Get a coal shovel, about a foot square, preferably with a short handle, and go to a steep hill. Straddle the shovel with the handle in front of you, grab the handle and lean back, and then hold on for dear life as you fly down the hill. It is really great! Of course our parents didn't appreciate us taking their shovels.

All this activity really packed the snow down. We put our barrel stave skis to the side and got that old refrigerator door and about six of us piled on. Riding this was similar to the snow saucers; you could not steer, and it went wherever it wanted to go. Sometimes it would go straight down the slope and other times it would be spinning around, zigzagging from side to side. We saw a group of kids pulling their sleds up the hill and we started yelling for them to get out of the way. We must have been going faster than the speed of sound because they acted like they didn't hear us and never moved. It was like getting a strike in bowling; kids and sleds went flying in all directions, some just wobbled back and forth and then fell over.

At the bottom of the graveyard was a dump where they threw all of the dead flowers, wreathes, and anything else they didn't want. It was overgrown with bramble bushes and small saplings. So when we got to the bottom, if we made it that far, we would either jump off or ride it into the dump. When we finally stopped, we would be so dizzy we would not be able to stand up for several minutes.

This was fun the first few days, but then our enthusiasm waned, and we got tired of pulling the heavy door up the hill. We would abandon the fridge door and eventually take it back to the dump to be covered over by the next day's trash.

We couldn't leave the door in the graveyard dump. The gravedigger, who lived two streets above the graveyard and always watched what we were doing, would yell at us to get it out of there. "It doesn't belong there," he would tell us.

I think he was a retired coalminer. He was short but muscular and I was always amazed that he could dig a six-foot deep grave in three hours, even in the winter when the ground was frozen solid. The sides would be perfectly straight and smooth. It was a work of art!

The following Monday school opened up again and all the roads were cleared of snow. Everything was returning to normal. This also meant that all of our fun was over. After supper I would get my sled, the one that could carry four kids sitting up. It must have been almost six feet long. Since my dad also grew up in the "Great Depression," he always thought that the bigger things were, the better. Like the year I got what he thought was a baseball and bat. He never played baseball when he was a kid, only soccer, so when he went to get the baseball and bat he got the biggest they had. They were a softball and a softball bat! When I went to the playground with these, no one would use them - they were way too heavy.

13

Before they went to bat they would pick up my softball bat and swing it a few times to warm up. Then when they picked up the baseball bat it felt as though it didn't weigh anything.

The Christmas that Santa brought me the sled, it had to be the biggest one he had. It was a "Speedaway" that must have been six feet long! If I rode this sled sitting up and was steering with my feet, if I wanted to make a turn, I would have to start fifty feet before the turn. Lying down was the only way I could ride this thing and I would drag my left foot to turn left and my right foot to turn right. We called this spragging, and snow would fly up on anyone who was behind me. They would yell, "Quit spragging, that's cheating!" but it was the only way I could steer.

I would go over to the graveyard to spend the evening sled riding. Sometimes I was the only one there. Just me and my gigantic sled. I would ride down the hill and pull the sled back up and I would do this all evening. I never got tired of it. I would make a jump out of snow and go over it with my sled and fly through the air and land with a violent jar onto the packed snow.

When I finally did go home, my mother would say, "You're going to get frostbite, you should come home once in a while to get a warm on." I knew once I came home I would not be allowed to go back out, so I would stay out as long as I could.

The weekend finally came around and I went to the graveyard to sled ride. I was the only one there and after a few runs down the hill, "smack" I got hit in the back with a snowball! "Hey Dandy, what are you doing?" Oh no, it was Joe. Trouble was sure to follow.

"I'm just sledding. What are you up to?"

"I'm going over to the pond, I hear it's frozen solid. Want to come?"

"Naw, I'll pass."

"They got some holes cut in the ice so you can fish. Come on, it'll be fun. You have been sledding for weeks now, aren't you tired of it?"

"I never get tired of this." Then I thought that this might be a way to add to my skills for when I go off to Canada. Ice fishing; nothing could go wrong!

"Come on!"

"Wait until I take my sled home and get some fishing line." I don't know what I was thinking; I had a bad feeling about all of this. But I sort of felt sorry for Joe; he didn't have any friends.

It had only been a little over a year since Joe's father had come home from his 3-11 shift as a 3rd helper at the open-hearth. He stopped at the Stumble Inn. As soon as you walked inside, the smell of stale beer would hit you. Then the smell of fresh sawdust, and tobacco juice that was in the trough between the foot rail and the bar that was used as a spittoon by the tobacco chewers would almost knock you over.

It was the tavern where they had that jar of pickled pigs feet on the bar. It was a clear, square jar with a red screw on lid. You could see the pigs' feet with the hooves still on them. That jar had been there ever since I could remember, and it didn't look like anyone had ever bought any. There was what appeared to be the same amount in the jar every time I went in there with my grandfather.

I didn't know if it was there for atmosphere or it was such a big seller and had to be refilled everyday. They didn't look very appetizing to me. My grandfather would take me there and we would go to the end of the bar and sit on the last stools. That was his seat and everyone knew not to sit there or there would be hell to pay. Then he would order a Pabst Blue Ribbon and I got Canada Dry Ginger Ale, or if they didn't have that, I would get a birch beer soda.

My grandfather had owned the bar previously and sold it to Jack with the stipulation that he could drink there for free. Jack had agreed, but under the condition that it was on the premises only, "NO take out." My grandfather reluctantly agreed. He was a retired coal miner and had owned a few mines in the area. Every time he sold a coalmine there was always a stipulation associated with it. He sold one to a local hardware store owner with the stipulation that he got a twenty percent discount on everything he bought there. With another mine he sold he would get free coal to heat his house. He was a good businessman.

Joe's father had a few quick beers and headed home. When he got there, he opened an Iron City beer, his favorite, and told his wife that he would be up when the "Creature Feature" with Chilly Willy was over. His father really enjoyed the classic horror movies of the 1930s

15

and 40s. That night they were having his favorite movie of all time - "Dracula" staring Bela Lugosi.

Bela had just died a few years ago, and Joe's father had told us that he had taken Bela's last wife, Hope, to the prom when they were in high school. His friends had dared him to ask Hope to the prom. They said she would never go out with the likes of him. "I dare you to ask Liny," her nickname, they had taunted him. So he did and she accepted; he said he couldn't believe it.

Apparently everyone else thought she was too good for them and nobody had asked her. She was too proud to ask someone to take her to the prom, so when he asked her, she didn't have to think twice and accepted. She really wanted to go to the prom, she didn't care who she went with. He only took her out that one time, but he said he could never forget her. She really had made an impression on him.

Then right after they graduated, she moved to California to find her fame and fortune. He would receive a Christmas card from her every year and she would always be bragging about all the movie stars she had met. She never did find her fortune, but in 1955 she wrote and told him that she had married "Dracula". Well, not actually "Dracula", but the star that portrayed "Dracula" in the movies.

She said that Bela was so fascinated with this role that he actually slept in a coffin. I could not believe this, but Joe's father said it was true and even showed us the letter. Sure enough, there it was in black and white on the one-page letter. Wow! To think this lady was from Johnstown and she did find fame.

Too bad it only lasted about a year. Bela Lugosi had died before they could celebrate their first anniversary together. She stayed in California and Joe's father did not get any more updates or cards from her. He said she just seemed to fall off the face of the earth after that.

He made a few trips to the refrigerator to get more beer during the commercials. He never went to bed. The Creature Feature must have been too much for him. Joe's mother found him sitting in his favorite chair with his beer still grasped in his hands, his eyes wide open, staring at the "test pattern" screen on the television at 2:00 in the morning. He had had a massive heart attack and never knew what hit him.

16

Joe never said anything to anyone, but I think he took it very hard and was now angry at the whole world. Before this he was just like everyone else and seemed to get along with everyone. Now it seemed as though he didn't care about anything.

I took my sled home and hurried back to the graveyard with a piece of fishing line and a lure in my pocket. Of course Joe was nowhere around. Then, "Whack!" I got hit on the back with a snowball, and from behind a tombstone I heard Joe laughing like crazy, which I think he was.

"You'll never learn, will you Dandy?"

"I knew I shouldn't go with you!"

"Come on, I won't throw any more snowballs."

So off we went to the pond. When we arrived there, there were about a dozen kids from Cookietown playing hockey with homemade sticks and no ice skates. Cookietown was at the bottom of Country Road where the valley was so deep and narrow that the sun did not shine there from October to March. It was a neighborhood made up of tar-paper shacks. I believe the people who first settled there were named Cook and that was how it got the name. They all had outhouses and some may have had electricity, but that is all. No one associated with these people; they were all a bunch of ruffians.

Luckily they were in a different school district, and my mother, as truant officer did not have to deal with them or she would have been there everyday. I had heard of people who drove through there and got a flat tire, but they would not stop to change it because they were too afraid of what might happen to them or their car. They just kept driving and ruined the tire and possibly the rim!

"Joe, lets get out of here! I don't want to go down there with them here."

"I know these guys, they're not that bad once you get to know them."

"You know these guys?"

"Oh yeah! I go to Cookietown all the time!"

Yes, Joe would fit in there. He was a lot like them. So we went down to the pond. Then I saw the holes had frozen over and there was no place to fish, not that I would have wanted to with these goons around. I just wanted to go home, but I didn't know what to

17

do. They all looked at us like we were freaks. Then Joe went over to the smallest guy there and grabbed his stick and shoved him into a snow bank and said, "Take a break, I'm going to use your stick for a while."

Then the biggest, ugliest goon there, with long, dirty, straggly blond hair sticking out from under his stocking cap, and warts on his face, ran toward Joe and started yelling, "Hey! That's my brother! I'm going to kill you!"

Then I could hear Joe yelling, "Take the damn stick, I don't want it!"

They pulled his coat up over his head and started pushing him from one to another. He looked like a ball in the pinball machine down at Kitz sub shop bouncing from a bumper to the flipper and back to the bumper. Then someone started screaming, "Get the other one!!"

That was all I needed to hear! I took off running and I just kept running faster and faster. The first rule, when someone is chasing you is don't run home, run in the opposite direction, you don't want them to know where you live. But in this case I just ran straight home, the sooner the better.

I didn't wait for Joe, but the next day I heard he had a black eye. He told everybody that he ran into a tree while skiing. Maybe he learned his lesson. We'll see!

Chapter 2

A few days after the pond incident, I ran into Joe. I saw him come out from behind a tree ahead of me. I stopped and turned around and started walking in the opposite direction. Then I heard him calling "Dandy! Hey Dandy, wait up!"

I stopped and turned around. His black eye was now fading to more of a lemon-yellow color. "What do you want? Every time I run into you, something bad happens."

"Nothing bad happened the last time I saw you."

"What do you mean nothing bad happened? When I left and ran home, you were dancing around with your jacket pulled up over your head and those goons from Cookietown were using you for a punching bag. I call that bad."

"They were just having fun, although I did get a black eye out of it, but that was an accident. In fact, that big guy, Gene, saved my life the other week."

"How on earth did he save your life? This I have to hear."

"When I told you there were holes in the ice, I am the one who made them, I wanted to be like one of those guys in the Polar Bear Club. So I made the holes in the ice and wanted to swim from one hole to the other. I took off all of my clothes and went in and...."

"Wait a minute! You took off all of your clothes? You must be crazy. What would people think if they saw you? And that water had to be cold!"

"There was nobody around the pond, I don't know how Gene saw me. And the water was warmer than the air, if you can believe that."

"No, I can't believe any of this. I think you are making it all up."

"Anyway, after I went in, I couldn't find the other hole and I couldn't find the one I just went in from. Gene must have seen me going in and he came over and saw me under the ice. There were about a six inch space between the ice and the water, so my head was above the water and I saw him pounding on the ice and motioning with his hand, so I followed his directions and went to the hole. So you see, those guys aren't so bad."

"Joe, you have one wild imagination! You don't expect me to believe all of that, do you?"

"Sure! It's the truth."

I never did find out if it was true or not, but with all the things that happened after that, I am inclined to believe him. That summer there were two carnivals in town at the same time. There must have been a mistake in scheduling, because no one would go to both; they appeared to have similar attractions. The volunteer fire companies in the area sponsored them as fundraisers. One was at the Guinea Field on "D" Street, and the other one was over at the Ten Acre on Tenth Avenue. It was late in the afternoon before the carnival opened up and I was walking around to see what kind of sideshows they had. I loved the smell of the carnivals, the cotton candy, the oil and grease, and the sawdust they had spread around the midway to cover the mud. This and not having to go to school were the only good things about summer.

I always thought that "they" should let us go to school in the summer and then have the winter off, whoever "they" were. We could be off from Thanksgiving at the end of November until the end of February. That way everyone could enjoy the whole winter. Boy, that would be GREAT! I doubted if they would do it before I finished school, at least Kindergarten had not been invented yet and I didn't have to attend that. Twelve years of school was enough!

There were the usual freak shows, red tents with white stripes and banners hanging above, and colorful signs stating: "The Wild Alligator Boy", "The Fat Lady", "The Tattooed Lady" her face and arms were covered by tattoos, and "The Beautiful Bearded Woman". They also had the usual "girly" shows, and then they had a weird show that stated a "Voodoo" guy would eat live chickens, feathers and all! Now this was one show I did not want to see.

I hurried past this one and who should come out from between two tents? None other than Joe! I was beginning to think he was stalking me. It seemed as though he turned up everywhere I went. Now what is going to happen? "Are you following me?"

"What gives you that idea?" Joe asked with a feigned look of surprise.

"Because you always turn up wherever I go, that's why."

"We must have a lot in common. I guess we're kindred spirits."

"I don't think so!" I said, amused at the thought.

"Sure we are, I think we should be best friends."

"We are friends, that is enough. You bring me bad luck."

"I can't help that, it's just a coincidence. I don't try to get into trouble."

"You just don't have any common sense Joe. If you do, you just don't care then."

"Whatever!" answered Joe in disgust.

I decided to change the subject, but as we walked past the tent with the large sign that read: "Madame Zelda Gypsy Fortune Teller" someone from inside of the tent hollered out in a broken English accent, "Hey boys, wait a minute."

Joe didn't hesitate and stopped dead in his tracks. I took a few more steps and then stopped and turned around to see what was going on.

A dark skinned woman with a large wart on her nose, dressed in a long black dress with gold colored designs and big, white, puffy sleeves, came out into the sunlight. She had a scarf wrapped around her head and there were what looked like gold coins dangling from it. She had it tied on the side in a big knot. Her long black hair was flowing out and ran half way down her back. There were large hoop earrings on her ears. She had numerous rings on her fingers and several bracelets on her arms. I was not sure if she dressed this way all the time or if it was because the carnival would be opening up soon.

I could hear her saying something to Joe and it sounded like she was talking in a foreign language. As I approached them she stopped talking to Joe and then asked, "Do you boys know where the other carnival is at Tenth Avenue?"

"I sure do," answered Joe with conviction.

"Yeah, we know where that is," I chimed in.

"Good! How would you like to make some money?"

My ears perked up. Money was high up on my list, right under going to Canada. I asked, "How much?" when I should have asked, "What do we have to do?"

"Fifty-cents a piece, or possibly a dollar."

21

"What do we have to do for half a buck or a dollar?" asked Joe, the first sensible thing I can remember him ever saying.

"I have a note I want you to take to my friend Anton, the "fire eater" over at the other carnival, and if you bring back an answer, I will give you another fifty-cents each."

This sounded like something in the movies, the Gypsy Fortune Teller and the Fire Eater passing notes back and forth. "Sure we can do that," I answered enthusiastically.

"Yeah, we can do that," replied Joe.

She already had the note made out, and she reached into her deep pocket and pulled it out along with a one-dollar bill. "Please take this over to him as quickly as you can, I need the reply soon."

"OK, we will be back as soon as we can," answered Joe as he put the money and the note in his pocket.

I think Zelda must have put a spell on Joe. He was starting to talk and act normal and was actually being polite. I hoped it lasted.

With the money and the note in Joe's pocket, we started running out of the carnival grounds past the penny pitch tent where you could win a plate, bowl, glass or whatever item the tossed penny stayed on. The glass was very shiny and colorful, with red, blue, yellow and pink iridescent colors. It was harder than it looked to win anything there. I think the items were waxed and the pennies slid right off when it landed on anything.

"We can slow down," I told Joe. "She can't see us now."

"If we want the other dollar, we have to get back to her as soon as possible," replied Joe. This didn't sound like him; this was something I would say.

"She will give us the money, it doesn't matter how long it takes us. She wants the answer to her note," I replied uncharacteristically.

We ran along the brick road by the railroad tracks and through the underpass and came out by the Ten Acre Bridge. This was a railroad bridge, not made for pedestrians, but people did use it as a shortcut to cross the river. It was a large steel arch bridge with railroad ties as the base. You would have to step on each tie to cross over. If you missed the tie, your foot would go between the ties and you would fall to the side. It was a dangerous practice, but everyone did it.

We were both out of breath now and started walking. I asked Joe, "What did that Gypsy say to you when she came out of the tent?"

"I don't know, she was talking in a foreign language that I couldn't understand. I know a little Slovak from my grandmother, but I didn't understand a word she was saying."

"I think she put a spell on you, Joe!"

"You're crazy, Dandy; you know that?"

"I'm serious Joe. You have been acting differently since we talked to her," I didn't want to tell him that he was being nice for a change.

"I'm acting the way I always do; it's you who is acting differently. Anyhow, there is no such thing as "spells" - you should know that."

"I hope you're right."

It took about fifteen minutes to get to Tenth Avenue. This carnival looked just like the other one, with the tents and the large colorful banners. We looked for the one advertising the "Fire Eater." About half way around the grounds we saw the banner: "Anton The World's Greatest Fire Eater" and "Samson the Strong Man." We were not only meeting a fire eater, but the world's GREATEST Fire Eater! Tubby would never believe this.

"Look, Joe! He's the Worlds Greatest Fire Eater."

"Yeah, right! Dandy, you believe anything don't you?"

"I don't believe anything YOU tell me, that's for sure."

We went into the tent and someone in the shadows started yelling: "Hey, you kids get out of here! You have to buy a ticket to come in here."

"The Gypsy over at the other carnival sent us here to see Anton!" I told the voice.

"Oh, is that right?" the voice asked.

"Yeah," said Joe.

"Why do you want to see Anton?"

"We have an important note from Zelda, the Gypsy lady," said Joe with authority.

"An important note you say," the voice moved from the shadows out into the dimly lit tent. He was the largest man I had ever have seen. He was wearing a white short sleeve pullover shirt and his muscles were bulging out on his arms and chest. He had boots on and tight fitting black pants. He turned and yelled back toward the shadows, "Hey, Anton, your "Old Lady" sent another love letter," in laughing voice.

Then, emerging from the darkness in the back of the tent, appeared a much smaller man. He was bare-chested and was wearing red tights. "Let me see it. I guess I better answer this one or she is going to keep sending more notes."

He read the note as he was laughing to himself. He then jumped up onto the stage and walked over to the podium and retrieved a pencil and a note pad and started writing. After a few minutes, he put the note into the envelope he had received. He pulled out four quarters and gave two of them to Joe along with the note. He then handed me two quarters and said, "Take this note back to the Gypsy. Tell her I won't need any more notes and don't wait for an answer."

"Will do, but could you show us how you eat fire?" asked Joe.

Anton, being the showmen that he was, walked over to a bucket that had a few metal rods with what looked like long corks on the end. He pulled a lighter out of his pocket with one hand, and with the other hand picked up a bottle filled with a liquid and took a drink from it. He set the bottle down and picked up one of the rods, put it in his mouth then took it out. Then, all in one motion with one hand, flicked open the lighter and lit it. That in itself was a sight to see. Then he lit the cork at the end of the rod.

He held the lit cork a few inches from his face and puckered up his lips and blew on the lit cork. The whole front of the tent lit up from the flames shooting out of his mouth and there was a loud roar like the sound of a blowtorch. I could feel the heat on my face and I was glad that I wasn't standing any closer to him.

I couldn't believe what I was seeing. I looked at Joe and he was really engrossed. He couldn't take his eyes off the sight. Anton blew on the lit cork a few times, the flames and roar became fainter each time. Then he put the burning cork into a bucket of water. The corked hissed and then he set it back in the bucket with the other rods.

"That's just gasoline!" hollered Joe.

"Yeah, so what," replied Anton.

"I could do that."

"Don't even try, you'll go up in flames and I don't want to have that on my conscience! Now get that note over to the Gypsy."

We ran out of the tent before Anton changed his mind and wanted his money returned. I could hear Anton yelling, "Don't you boys even think about doing this!"

"We're going to make a buck fifty for an hours work," I told Joe. "That's the most money I ever made."

"Yeah, and I learned how to be a fire eater! That's the best part," replied Joe enthusiastically.

The carnival grounds were opening up now. As we walked by the "Bearded Lady" sideshow, the barker started up his chant, "Hey gentlemen, come on in, only ten cents, one thin dime, 1/10 of a dollar gets you through the door. For 25 cents see a little more!"

We just shook our heads side to side and kept on walking. "Come on in, she won't bite, I promise," yelled the barker.

We finally made it back to the Gypsy Fortune Teller's tent and she was standing outside trying to persuade prospective customers to come inside to have their fortunes told. When she saw us, she stopped her spiel and motioned for us to hurry over.

"Give me the note," she hollered. Then the Gypsy took the note and opened it up and her lips started moving as she read it silently to herself.

She then suddenly stopped reading, her eyes rolled back into her head, and she tilted her head back. I thought she was going to black out. Then she started chanting in a foreign language and it sounded like she was repeating the same thing over and over. Her voice started getting louder, and she started to tremble all over. People were stopping and watching the spectacle. Women that were walking past with little children grabbed their hands and hurried them by in fright.

I didn't know whether to get out of there or wait for the money. I thought for sure a bolt of lightning was going to shoot down from the sky and strike us all. I kept hoping that nobody I knew saw me there. Joe couldn't take his eyes off the sight.

Then Zelda slowly lowered her head and opened her eyes. They were as big as half dollars, and she smiled. Just then the fire siren at the volunteer fire company sounded and all of the volunteer fireman started running for their cars to get to the firehouse. Then she realized we were still there.

"Lets see, I owe you a dollar, don't I?"

"You sure do," replied Joe.

"You better change your ways, my son," she said while looking straight into Joe's eyes and handing me the money.

Neither of them moved for what seemed an eternity, but it must have only been a few seconds. She started chanting again in a foreign language, and then turned and disappeared into the shadows of her tent.

Joe just stood there not moving a muscle.

"Joe, come on. Let's get out of here," I told him.

He acted as though he didn't hear me and just stood there staring into space. I finally grabbed his arm and tried to pull him away.

"Joe, come on. What's the matter with you?"

He was stumbling and dragging his feet and then all of a sudden he said, "Hey, quit pulling me. I can walk."

"Then start walking. What's wrong with you? Did she put a spell on you?"

"Yeah, right!"

"Well, something is wrong with you!"

"You're crazy Dandy. That's what you are. I am going to buy some gas with my money and become a fire eater."

"Didn't you hear what that Gypsy told you? You better change your ways."

"I will! I'm going to be a fire eater."

"I don't think that's what she meant."

The next morning as I was eating my Quaker Puffed Rice, my mother came into the kitchen reading the newspaper. She sat down, flicked her cigarette ashes into an ashtray, and said, "Oh my, there was a fire at the Tenth Avenue carnival last night."

I almost choked on my cereal. This couldn't be real, it had to be a coincidence. I hope it had nothing to do with the fire eater!

"It says here: As Anton the fire eater was preparing for his act and putting on a promotional show in front of the tent to draw in customers, the wind changed direction and caught one of the banners on fire. If it weren't for the quick action of the local volunteer firemen, it could have been a catastrophe. As it turned out, only a small portion of the tent was damaged and the show went on as scheduled."

"So nobody was hurt," I replied.

26

"No, just minor damage. I don't want you going down to the carnivals, they are not safe. Especially those rides. They tear them down one day and put them up the next, those nuts and bolts have to be wearing out from all of that. You never know when something is going to break. And all of those weird carnie people. I heard that there is some bizarre character there that eats LIVE chickens! He went into the Stumble Inn and ordered their best Scotch. Jenny, the barmaid, asked him why he eats live animals and then comes in there and orders the best they have, and he said "When I drink, I only get top shelf." He finished his drink and left. She said he was the strangest guy she ever had met. Just don't go down there."

"Aw, there is nothing else to do around here in the summer. Can't I go down if I don't ride on any rides?"

"Well, just don't go alone and don't go on any rides."

"I won't go alone, and I don't like going on the rides anyway, you know that. Ever since we went on that ride last year and it stayed upside down the whole time. That was the last ride I ever went on. I guess I will have to get Tubby or Andy to go with me."

"As long as it isn't Joe, you know what I think of him."

"Yeah, me too!" I hope she doesn't find out about last night, I thought.

That Gypsy must have put a curse on Anton; it couldn't have been a coincidence. I wondered how Joe was making out.

A few days later I had been riding my bike all day and I never saw Tubby, Andy or anyone else from the neighborhood. It was a hot day and everyone must have gone swimming or were staying in the house. I didn't like to swim; I went to Fichtner's once to swim and almost drowned. There was a pier out in the middle of the pool and you had to swim to get there. Well, I didn't know how to swim, so I just started walking and didn't realize the bottom of the pool was level for six feet, and then sloped down to twenty feet! It was slimy on the bottom and when I hit the sloped section I started to slide. The lifeguards were too busy watching all the girls and didn't notice me going under. Luckily there was someone close by and I grabbed onto them and pulled myself up. They didn't appreciate it, but they did save my life. I never returned to Fichtner's again.

I decided to take a walk out past the Indian Caves since it was getting too hot to ride my bike. These were not really caves and they were not made by Indians. That was just an urban legend. Kids would find triangular pieces of stone and think they were Indian arrowheads. It was an area dug out years ago for the shale and a pathway went by the area untouched by the digging, so it was sort of secluded and could not be seen from the trail.

As I got closer to the caves I could hear a roar. This sounded familiar and I was trying to think where I had heard this sound before. Then I saw the leaves on the trees above the caves turn an orange color each time I heard the roar. I then realized that it sounded like Anton the fire eater!

I ran through the bushes and up over to the top of the bank and looked down into the Indian Caves. There was Joe, all alone, with a bottle of gasoline, being a fire eater! He was doing it just like Anton. He took a mouthful of gasoline and had a straightened out metal coat hanger with a rag wrapped around one end and he lit it with a cigarette lighter. He could not do it one handed like Anton, but he did everything else like him. The flames shot out of his mouth with a roar and everything lit up. "This would really be a sight at night," I thought to myself.

I didn't want to yell to Joe; I was afraid I might disturb his concentration, and he might get hurt. At least the area is sunk down and the wind does not blow through it. That is all Joe would need, a big gust of wind coming from the wrong direction. I would not want to be a witness to that.

I watched roar after roar until Joe ran out of gasoline. I then went down as Joe threw the empty glass pop bottle and it shattered against the stone wall of the caves.

"What are you doing, Joe?"

"Where did you come from? How long have you been here?" asked Joe with an embarrassed look on his face.

"I was up there watching for a few minutes," I replied, pointing to the top of the caves.

"I know what I want to do when I get out of school. I am going to join the carnival and be a fire eater."

"You're not serious, are you?"

"Yeah, I am. There is nothing to this fire eater stuff - it's easy. I will get paid and I will get to see the world, too."

"I am not sure if you will get to see the world, you could see other parts of this country, though. I wouldn't want to be traveling all over the country. I just want to stay in one place."

"Not me. I get tired of the same thing everyday. I want to travel and I would not have to work hard. This fire eater stuff is really easy."

"It's dangerous, Joe. Look at what happened to Anton. He almost burned the tent down and he could have gotten burned, too."

"I think that Gypsy put a curse on him. I don't know what that note was about, but she didn't seem too happy after she read it."

"Joe, I can't believe you said that. I thought you didn't believe in spells and curses."

"Dandy, I think she put a spell on me that day. Remember you asked me what was wrong; I just didn't feel the same for a few days after that. I didn't want to do anything, just sit around the house. Then today it seemed as though I came out of a fog. I remembered Anton and this was the first thing I wanted to do in days, so I did it! I am going to join the carnival. Want to come with me?"

"NO! But when you do, keep me posted as to where you are."

That was the adventure of that summer. I will never forget it as long as I live. Joe did keep practicing his fire-eating skills. Other people saw him at the Indian Caves spewing fire from his mouth. One of the goons from Cookietown tried it and the first and only time he did it, the wind changed directions and he looked as though he had a sun burnt face. He was lucky it wasn't worse. Now Joe is regarded as some sort of a "god" in Cookietown because he can do this and they can't.

Did Joe go swimming like the people with the Polar Bear Club? I believe he did. He says he did and he was crazy enough to do it. I would have asked the goon from Cookietown that saved his life, but there was a rumor going around that he left town and joined a circus. He was now a clown with a big red nose and big floppy shoes and bright red wig in a too big yellow and white costume. That would be an improvement over what he actually looked like. Whatever he did, he was never seen or heard from again. Maybe that is where Joe got the idea to join the carnival.

Chapter 3

It was now near the end of January and my mother thought we should be getting the "January thaw" soon. She said there were always a few days when the weather would turn warm and the snow would start melting. This is not what I wanted to hear. I may have to leave for Canada soon.

When my father built the cement block foundation that we lived in, he had heard that you could get a house from the Sears Roebuck catalog. Then he found out they discontinued them. Now he was looking into all of his options. He wanted to get the house started soon because last fall when the tail end of a hurricane came through, our flat roof started leaking.

I remember the day very clearly; it was a Monday evening in October and I had gone to get my hair cut at John's Barber Shop. John had a day job and only cut hair in the evenings. I had told him I wanted to let my sideburns grow longer and not to cut them short.

"You're not going to be looking like one of those Rock and Rollers like Elvis, or one of those Beatniks! I'll trim them to the middle of your ear, the same as everyone else," he lectured me as he cut my hair.

I didn't want to resemble Elvis, but I did like the Beatnik look. But I ended up with my usual flattop haircut. John had a thin board that looked like a large wooden comb with a bubble level on it to make sure my haircut was straight and level. I looked like I was in the army at basic training.

My mother had told me to come straight home after getting my haircut because there was a storm coming. As I left the shop I noticed the sky was a pea green. I had never seen it that color before. The wind was blowing violently, the trees were bending over and the few remaining leaves were blowing off them. The wind was picking up the leaves and dirt, and they were swirling up into small cyclones. I started running and it started to rain, then it came down in buckets. I was soaked by the time I got in the door.

As I ran inside I could see my father running through the rooms with buckets and bowls yelling, "Blimey, there's another leak.

30

Fiddlesticks! Here's another." There were buckets, pans, cans and bowls everywhere with water dripping into them. My mother and father spent the whole week emptying all those containers. I could not remember it raining for such a long period of time. I couldn't go outside until Friday evening when it finally stopped raining. That was the longest time I had ever spent indoors. I hate rain, there is no worse feeling than getting drenched in the rain.

That was when my father said we could not spend another year in that foundation. There was an ad in the newspaper from a local contractor that said they would build the shell of the house and the homeowner could finish the inside. He had called them and they were coming to talk about it.

I was in my bedroom playing with my Robin Hood Castle set when there was a knock at the door and a guy in a suit was let into the house. I heard them talking about different things, but my father kept saying, "Now, I am just looking into this and I am not going to make a decision yet. There are a few more people I want to talk to first. So I don't want you to start on this yet."

The guy in the suit replied, "If you hear anything on the roof, it will just be the birds." And then he left.

The next morning we were all awakened by loud noises and scraping sounds on the roof. My father yelled, "Fiddlesticks! That's not birds!" and ran outside to find a few men unloading wood onto our foundation roof to start putting up the shell of the house! He ran back inside and called the guy in the suit and told him, "Get your birds off my roof, now!"

That spring after the weather broke and most of the snow had melted, we took a drive to New Alexandria where they had model homes on display. My father kept talking about Lincoln Homes. I knew Lincoln grew up in a log cabin, so I thought these must be log homes. That would be great. I would really like living in a log house.

It was a dreary day with fog and rain. We had to go over the Penn View Summit and it was so foggy you could not see anything past the hood of the car. My mother and father both opened their doors and were watching the lines on the road to make sure we did not go off the road. I just kept hoping that no one stopped in front of us because we would not know it until we ran into them. Luckily we made it over the summit and started down the other side and it was as if someone lifted a blanket off of the car. The fog disappeared in an instant.

We made it through to New Alexandria. There were several companies on both sides of the road with model homes. My father heard that Lincoln homes had a house that would fit on our foundation.

When my father built the foundation, he was not thinking about what size to make it. He was planning to build the house himself, so it didn't matter what the size was. Then he decided to get a Sears Craftsman House, but as I mentioned, they stopped making them. Then he heard about the new "prefab" houses that were being made. Well, these prefab houses only came in certain sizes and he had to find one to fit the foundation he built.

We found the Lincoln Homes site with all types of model homes, but no log homes that I could see. From Ranch homes to Cape Cods, I never knew the difference until that day. We were shown through Colonial and Cottage style homes, and many other styles that I can't remember. Finally my father said, "Fiddlesticks! Look, here is the size of my foundation. Just show me the houses that will fit on it."

The salesman took the paper with the dimensions, "Why didn't you show me this before? We only have one home this size. It's a story and a half, three bedroom Cape Cod."

"Let's go have a look see," replied my father happily. I think he was starting to worry that he would never find a house to fit the foundation.

There it was, a green-sided house, which looked just like half of the other houses in our neighborhood.

"I'll take it!" yelled my father, glad that the ordeal was almost over.

"Once you get the financing, we can have it set up on your foundation in one day. This model is $4,995. That includes all the kitchen cupboards, doors, windows, sheetrock, electrical wiring, everything to finish the inside. It does not include the furnace or appliances. We can finish the whole house for that price, or if you want to do some work yourself, we can reduce the price somewhat. It all depends how much you want to do."

"How much would the price be if you just finish the first floor and I finish the second?"

We were in the office and the salesman had a big calculator with a large handle on the side that he pulled after entering numbers on the keypad. After punching the keys and several pulls of the handle he said, "We can let you have the Cape Cod for $4,495."

My father thought about this for a few minutes. The salesman just sat there. He didn't say a word. Finally my dad said, "OK, it's a deal."

They shook hands and the salesman said, "Call us when you have the financing in place," and he handed him his card with the phone number on it.

We left the office and walked by the Cape Cod for one last look. Then we got in the car and headed home. My mother was not sure we were doing the right thing.

"We are going to be in debt for 20 or 30 years," she sobbed.

"Don't worry, we will be OK," replied my father.

"Well at least you saved ten percent by doing the upstairs yourself."

"Yes, that should not take too long to finish. But first we have to go to the bank to get a loan."

"I guess they will give us one, don't you think so?"

"I am sure they will. I am working and we have some money for a down payment. We shouldn't have any problem getting the money."

They did get the loan, and within a month our house arrived on a long truck with a big boom that lifted the sides of the house off the truck and onto our foundation. My father had the day off when they came with the house. We stood outside and watched as the workmen attached cables to the house sides and hoisted them off of the truck and onto the foundation.

They started with the back wall. It had all the windows and siding already attached. They swung it over and braced it up with 2x4's so it would not fall over. Then they swung one end with the kitchen door and windows in it over to the end and started attaching it to the back wall.

All of a sudden my father jumped up and started waving his arms while yelling, "Fiddlesticks! That wall goes on the other end of the house, NOT that end. We will have our steps in the neighbors yard if you put it there. The kitchen is on the other end of the house."

The workman just raised his hand to let my father know that he heard him. They pulled out the nails they had started putting in and moved it to the other end of the house. An hour or so later they had all four walls up then they put the interior walls in. These were just the bare studs and it didn't take long for these. Then they put in the second story floor, then the two gable ends and the roof. It already had the shingles and dormers on it. All they had to do was put the cap on the roof ridge and the aluminum corners on the siding. They did all of this in one day.

The next day another crew came and started working on the inside of the house. They ran the electrical wiring and put in the ceiling lights and outlets. After the electrical and plumbing was finished they put up the sheetrock for the walls. While this was all going on, there was another crew putting in the kitchen cabinets and hanging the interior doors. When they were done that day, all that my father had to do was paint the walls and varnish the doors and floors and finish the upstairs.

After a few weeks, we were ready to move upstairs. My father had used knotty pine for my bedroom and it looked like the inside of a log cabin. I was elated, I finally got to live in a log cabin! Being up on the second floor, I could look out over the valley below. I also had a great view of the woods and graveyard, too. Life was good. I might not have to move to Canada.

Chapter 4

February ended the January thaw. It started snowing again and got colder. Tomorrow was Groundhog Day and Punxsutawney Phil, up on Gobbler's Knob, better see his shadow! Then we will have six more weeks of winter. I could hear my father now, "Fiddlesticks! That's all a bunch of poppycock. Six weeks from today, it will be the first day of spring, whether he sees his shadow or not!"

My father thought this was all a lot of nonsense, all these people standing out in the cold waiting for a large rodent to come out of his burrow in zero degree weather. Then the Grand Sage of the Inner Circle would hold Phil up and he would whisper in his ear whether it would be a "long winter" or an "early spring." Then he would run back in his burrow, wouldn't you?

Phil did see his shadow and there will be six more weeks of winter! Yea!! In another week on the second Sunday of February the Stump Creek Sportsman's Club would have their yearly "game feed." The National Guard would supply the trucks and drivers and the sportsmen would load the trucks with bags of corn. Then they would drive up into the mountains and put the corn out for the animals. The snow was always the deepest this time of year, and the animals would have a hard time finding food. This would help them make it through the long winter.

The week before this, my father and I, and "Deadeye," another club member, were going to a farm over in Ryot to get the corn. Deadeye had a five-ton dump truck that he used to deliver coal when he was laid off from the mill. He was a luterman at the Coke Plant. He sealed up the coke oven doors with mud. I knew all this because that was all he talked about as we made the two-hour trip. I was becoming an expert on Coke Plant operations. I think if I worked there, I would want to operate the pusher. This sounded better than the other jobs like "lidman, larry car operator, coal handler, tar chaser, and mudman". Yes, I knew them all after this trip. The way he described the Coke Plant, I could almost smell the place. He said it smelled like a barrel of sauerkraut gone bad with a few dozen rotten eggs thrown in to it.

Deadeye was liked by everyone. Well, I imagine almost everyone; I am sure some of the people he pulled his pranks on did not appreciate him. He was a war hero, storyteller, great hunter and fisherman, and above all, the greatest prankster of all time!

Just then I thought I could hear someone off in the distance, calling, "Danny! Danny!" but I couldn't see anyone. It sounded like it was coming from Cookietown. Those guys over there would not know that I was called Dandy now. I hoped they were not coming after me because of what happened at the pond last month.

Then my father started laughing uncontrollably! I had no idea what was so funny. Then I heard it again, "Danny! Danny!" Then Deadeye started laughing; he couldn't control himself. I knew then that something was up. As it turned out he could throw his voice without moving his lips and he was an expert. He really had me going.

"You should have seen the look on your face. I thought you heard a ghost or something," hollered Deadeye while laughing at the same time. He didn't know I thought those goons were coming after me. Well, at least everyone else was in a good mood.

"Johnny," (that's what everyone called my father, it was short for "Johnny Bull" - it was like saying "Uncle Sam",) "did I ever tell you about the time I went to Akron to work when we were laid off here?" asked Deadeye.

"Oh, I heard you were working in a lorry factory," answered my father.

"No, not a lorry factory; I don't even know what a lorry is. No, I was working at a place that made truck beds. I was living with my sister and her husband and I got a job there. Well anyway, this place wasn't unionized and we didn't make a lot of money. So I told the owner that if he didn't give us a raise, I was going to pull the main breaker to the place and we were all walking out."

"What happened?" asked my father.

"Well, the owner said if I pulled the switch, I would be fired."

"And then what did you do?"

"I pulled the switch, what do you think I would do?"

"Did you get the raise?"

36

"No, he fired me and I had to find a job somewhere else. Luckily, I got called back to work here."

"I thought you were going to tell me you all got a big raise! That is how most of your stories end."

"Well, no happy ending for this one, except, like I said, shortly after that I did get recalled to the Coke Plant."

"I don't know how you can work in that dirty, stinking place."

"Oh, you get used to the smell after a while. I don't even notice it anymore. Did I ever tell you about the time I killed two deer with one arrow?"

"Only about ten times," answered my father wincingly.

"I didn't hear about it. How could you get two deer with one arrow?" I asked him.

"I was walking along Horse Hill and working my way up to the top. When I got up there, I saw a deer just over the ridge. I like to shoot them in the neck, so I don't ruin the meat. Well when I let the arrow go, the deer must have heard me and raised its head up and the arrow just nicked the vein in its neck. I didn't even see the second deer behind the first until it raised its head. The arrow then kept going and got the other deer right in the heart. They both fell over dead. That was how I got two deer with one arrow."

"I don't believe it. Is this just another story you made up?" I asked him.

"Luckily Big John was there and he saw it too, or else no one would believe me."

"Wow, so you did shoot two deer with one arrow. That is something."

How come everyone else has a great nickname and I get stuck with "Dandy"? We drove on in silence the remainder of the time. I could not believe I was in the company of this great hunter and storyteller. This was a day I would not forget.

The farm was a nice neat place on a flat area with the mountain in the background. The house was painted white and the barn was red with a large "Chew Mail Pouch Tobacco" sign on the side facing the road.

At the farmhouse we met Joe Nature, his wife, and his son Pete. Joe and his son got on a green John Deere farm tractor, and we followed behind them over to the barn to get the bags of corn.

Joe and Pete were pushing on the huge barn doors to get them opened, when I heard someone calling, "Hey Joe!"

Joe and Pete both looked toward the house and Joe started yelling: "What do you want?" No answer. A few seconds later we heard it again, "Hey Joe!"

Joe hollered again: "What do you want?" again, no answer.

"Hey Joe!"

"WHAT!!"

"You forgot your hanky!"

"That woman has gone crazy!" Joe told us. "Does she think I'm going to go all the way back to the house for my hanky?" Then he reached in his back pocket and pulled out the biggest handkerchief I ever saw and started waving it in the air, "See, I got it! Now leave me alone."

Deadeye figured he better quit before Joe lost his cool. Joe never did find out what had happened and he probably gave his wife an earful when he got home. I hope they didn't get divorced over this. We filled the truck with the bags of corn and left for home.

The ride home was uneventful. We did stop for coffee, and I had a bottle of pop. Deadeye asked me if I wanted milk. I told him I didn't drink milk anymore since the time I had to take 'milk pills'! Now I think he thought I was pulling one over on him.

"What are 'milk pills'?" he asked.

"Well, I got pneumonia a few years ago, and I had to take these pills every morning. My mom said they were 'milk pills' that I had to take with my milk. Well, they tasted terrible and I dreaded every morning, because I had to take these pills. After a few days, I was done taking the pills and I wouldn't drink milk ever again!"

Deadeye started laughing and said, "They weren't 'milk pills', that was penicillin that you were taking."

"I don't care what it was, I can't drink milk anymore!"

My father just sat there. He had heard this story many times and he didn't think it was amusing anymore. I know he was thinking, "Fiddlesticks! That's a lot of poppycock!'

The day before the game feed I went over to Tubby's house to ask him if he wanted to go on the game feed with me. My dad didn't want me going alone. He would stay at the clubhouse and help load the corn onto the trucks. He was afraid I might get lost up on the mountain, and he thought that if I were with someone I knew, we would stay together. He was probably right.

"Now why would I want to go trudging though snow up to my waist on the mountain?" asked Tubby.

"'Because when we come back to the clubhouse, after we're done, we can have all the kielbasa, hot dogs, sauerkraut, and pop that we want, and I know you like to eat!" I told him.

"Yeah, that might be a good reason, but it is going to be zero or colder tomorrow."

"They have trucks to take us up there, we don't have to walk up the mountain."

"But we will have to carry the corn to put it out."

"Come on, it'll be fun. Anyhow, you know Deadeye?"

"Yeah, he brings the coal to our house every year. My old man says he's a big bag of wind and you can't believe anything he says. He's just a big storyteller."

"Maybe, but he said that he and a few other guys built a log cabin up on top of Laurel Mountain and they named it Deerlick. If we go with him tomorrow, he'll take us there."

"Yeah, I've heard of that place. I would like to see it. Then we could go inside and get warm and we won't freeze to death! You know, it's always ten degrees colder up there than down here."

"That, and with all that food, you'll do it, right?"

"Yeah, I'll go with you. I hear your old man is going to build a house on your foundation. My old man says he wouldn't buy anything big while there's a republican in the White House. My mom wanted a new stove and fridge, but he wouldn't buy them. So she went and painted the ones we have to cover up all the nicks and scratches. We only had black paint so she painted them black. It's not so bad after a while, you get used to them. My old man said my mom saved him a couple hundred dollars by painting them."

"Your dad sure is a cheapskate! But I will say one thing, when he does buy something, it's always the best - like that Schwinn Black Phantom bike with the big spring on the front."

"Yeah, that is a good bike! But, he likes to be debt free, as he calls it. He doesn't want to have to depend on anyone for anything, that's why he won't switch to gas from coal."

"He has to depend on the coalminers for coal; what if they go on strike?"

"That's why he gets his coal in the summer when it's cheaper. The miners never strike in the summer, only after the weather turns cold. Anyhow, the small mines are family-owned and they don't strike. With gas, he says you also need electricity to run the furnace, so you're dependent on the gas company AND the electric company. Naw, he'll never switch, and that's also why we have that big garden and all those chickens. We'll have vegetables and eggs and never starve no matter what happens. My mom spends all summer canning. She hates it though."

"That's how I'm going to be when I go to Canada - not be dependent on anyone!"

"Are you still thinking about going to Canada? You'll never go. You wouldn't last a week there, anyway."

"Oh yeah, you'll see, as soon as I get out of school, I'm going. I'm saving my money now to buy traps and snowshoes and things like that. A good sturdy axe and a sharp knife, that's all I'll need."

"Yeah? Well, you might need some pots and pans, too. Don't forget to send me a postcard when you go to the "trading post" to pick up provisions."

"Very funny. You'll see! Hey, don't forget to be at my house at 7:30 tomorrow morning."

"7:30?? On a Sunday?? You must be kidding, that's my day to sleep in!"

"Just be there! I'll see you tomorrow."

The next morning after eating a hearty breakfast, there was a loud yelling from outside, "Hey Daaandy! Hey Daaandy!" It was Tubby calling me.

"Why can't your mates just knock on the door like civilized people?" asked my father.

"Because we just go to each others house and call them, that is the way it is done." I replied.

"Fiddlesticks! I never heard of such an idiotic custom!"

I ran to the door and let Tubby in. The wind was howling and the snow was blowing horizontally, the temperature was about zero. It seemed as though there was always a snowstorm around this time of February.

"I'll wait in the car," said Tubby.

"We're not taking the car, we're going to hike over to the club," my father chimed in.

"Hiking?? In this weather? Maybe I'll just go home," Tubby said and started to turn around.

"I don't want to get the car stuck somewhere and have to leave it there, so we will just walk over. You'll be fine," assured my father.

"Then they better have lots of kielbasa afterwards!" he mumbled as he returned to the room.

"Oh they will, I am helping them cook it. They ordered over fifty pounds of kielbasa and hot dogs."

The three of us set out for the club. It was so cold that the snow didn't just crunch when we walked on it, but it squeaked as well. The leaves on the Mountain Laurel were curled up and looked like green pencils dangling from the branches. I kept waiting for Tubby to start complaining, but he never did. If my father hadn't been there, I'm sure he would have been complaining the whole time.

It would take about twenty minutes to get there if we took the shortcut down the hill and across Stump Creek, if it was frozen over. Otherwise it would take another ten minutes to get to the bridge to cross the creek. We looked for an area where the water was calm and it was frozen over.

The snow was really coming down and I was afraid they would cancel the game feed, but my father said they would never cancel it. He said those army trucks could go anywhere in any type of weather conditions.

We finally made it to the club. It had once been a one-room schoolhouse and they had replaced all of the windows with smaller ones. There was now a bar where the teachers' desk would have been, and there were mounted birds and animals on all of the walls. Behind the bar there was a large wooden sign that my father had painted. It pictured a hunter and a bird dog, with a pheasant being flushed out and the dog pointing. Above the sign it read: "Stump Creek Trap & Field Club."

I remember my father working on that sign when we lived at Ducky Beach. He had the large pieces of plywood leaning up against the wall in the kitchen. That was the only area where he had enough room to work on it. He had newspapers scattered around so he wouldn't get any paint on the floor. My mother kept telling him, "Get that thing out of here." He had that sign done in record time.

I made sure Tubby and I got on the truck with Deadeye; I really wanted to go to see this log cabin called "Deerlick." There were six of us in the back of the truck sitting on the wooden slats of the fold-down benches on each side, and the bags of corn were piled up in the middle of the truck. Deadeye was up front with the driver. He was probably telling him all about his job at the Coke Plant.

Tubby spit on the metal floor of the truck and it froze instantly.

"Did you see that?" yelled Tubby. "That spit froze as soon as it hit the floor!"

I told Tubby, "Well, don't spit on the floor then."

"I knew I should have stayed home. We will probably freeze to death up here and they won't find our bodies until spring!" The four other older guys start laughing.

"All we have to do is put this corn out and then we can go to the cabin."

"What do you mean all we have to do? That's enough."

"Once you start moving, you'll be warm."

The truck veered off of the road and started to ascend the gas line. That was where the natural gas line came across the mountain into the city. No vehicles were allowed on it, but the club got a special permit to drive up there once a year. The first part was very steep where it came down to the headwaters of Stump Creek.

The truck driver stopped and put the truck in low gear and then started up the steep hill. We made it to the top of that ridge where it more or less leveled off for a while and then we started up the next hill to the top of that ridge. The summit, according the sign, was over twenty-five hundred feet above sea level.

We finally stopped and Deadeye got out and came around and let the tailgate down. We threw all the bags of corn out of the truck onto the snow. There were also some wire baskets made out of chicken wire that would be nailed onto trees in the area and filled with the corn. The snow must have been four feet deep up there on the mountain. It had a thick crust that you could walk on without breaking through into the deep snow. At least I could walk on it. Tubby and the adults couldn't; they kept breaking through and it took them forever to walk a few feet. Every now and then one of my feet

42

would break through the snow and I would fall over on my side. I could see what they had to put up with.

After a few minutes of trying to walk through this, Deadeye said there was no way we could go into the woods with the snow this deep. He told us to load the corn back onto the truck and had the driver drive us up to Deerlick.

"Take the corn off the truck, put the corn back onto the truck... I am getting tired of this," said Tubby.

Deadeye had the driver drive the truck around the cabin several times to pack the snow down. Then he nailed the baskets onto the trees around the cabin and we filled them up. He said he never saw the snow that deep before, and he wondered how the other groups were making out.

After all the corn was put out, we went into the cabin. It was just as I had imagined. It had a wood burning stove and Deadeye made a fire in it while we were putting out the corn, so it was nice and warm when we went inside.

There were even two sets of bunk beds at the far end of the room. It was about sixteen feet wide and twenty feet long with a window on the south side and one on the eastern side. There was a huge coffee pot, blue with white specks, brewing on the stove and it smelled great. I could live in a place like this! I didn't want to leave.

Tubby couldn't wait to leave. He wanted to get back to the club to get some food, and he said he didn't drink coffee. After everyone got warm, we got into the truck and headed back down the mountain. It didn't take as long to go down as it did to come up. We finally arrived back at the club. Tubby was the first one out and he ran into the building. By the time I got in there he already had half a kielbasa sandwich eaten; he sure didn't waste any time. He must have eaten six of them while we were there. I was getting sick just watching him eat. I don't know how he did it.

Deadeye gave us a ride home, which made Tubby very happy. I don't think he could have walked that far without getting sick. That was the game feed for that year, and I was sure glad I went and got to see the inside of a real log cabin. Now when I go to Canada, I will know how to build my cabin. It will look just like Deerlick.

We got back to normal routine after the game feed. The refrigerator door was lying at the bottom of the graveyard waiting to be taken to the dump after the snow melted. Everyone was content riding sleds or skiing. Of course Tubby had the best sled I ever saw. I don't know why he wanted the refrigerator door. That Duralite sled was not the usual red frame and runner with wooden deck; it was silver-color frame and runners with a wooden deck. The rear runner ran about three quarters of the way to the front, and then the front quarter runner was separate and would turn independently from the rear and had a spring on the mechanism that would bring it back to center after turning. That thing could do a ninety-degree turn - I never saw anything like it.

"How come you hardly ever get out that sled?" I asked Tubby.

"'Cause my old man doesn't want anyone to know that I have it. I only ride it when he's not home."

"Why? That's a great sled!"

"Yeah, but it's not made of steel; it's made of aluminum."

"So what difference does that make?"

"Well you should know, since your old man works in the mill, too."

"Know what?"

"That if you work in the mill you only buy stuff that is made out of steel, and not "imported" steel, like those German VW Beetle cars that you see everywhere."

"What's that got to do with your sled?"

"We don't make aluminum here in Johnstown, that's what."

"Oh, I see."

"My old man says we make all the sled runners here in the eight inch mill. No one else makes it anywhere in the world! He didn't realize this sled was made of aluminum or he wouldn't have bought it. Did you hear about the guy that bought a plastic lunch bucket?"

"No."

"Well, he bought a plastic lunch bucket and the first day he took it to work, someone set a hot slab near it and it melted flat as a pancake! The guy that put the slab there said he didn't see the bucket, but everyone knows different. If you work in the steel mill, you buy American steel, not German, not aluminum, and not plastic. By the way, did you get asked to the Sadie Hawkins Day Dance?"

"Are you crazy? I wouldn't go even if I was asked," I replied.

44

"Why not?"

"That's the last thing I'd want to do. That would be worse than going to the dentist! I just want to go to Canada and...."

"Yeah, yeah, I know, build a log cabin by a deserted lake. You'll never do that, so come down to earth and forget about it."

"Oh yes I will! That's my goal in life. That's all I want. You'll see, I'll do it! Are you going to the dance?"

"I'm not telling."

"Who would ask you?'

"Like I said, I'm not telling."

"You're not going."

"You'll never know, since you're not going. You'll have to come to the dance to see who I go with, smarty."

"I could care less." With that I took a running start and jumped onto my six foot Speed-Away sled and Tubby took off after me. We spent the rest of the day riding down the hill and pulling our sleds back up.

The next day when I got up, they were calling for a blizzard on the radio. That would be great! I put on my winter gear, boots, scarf, coat, leather mittens, and ski mask and headed up the hill into the woods.

It started snowing - flurries at first, then when I got to the top of the hill, the snow really started coming down hard and the wind started blowing. The wind blew the snow over everything and it looked like someone took a spray gun and sprayed snow on all the trees and bushes. It looked like a Christmas card; it was beautiful.

But then it started snowing even harder, I never saw anything like it. I had heard of people saying that they couldn't see their hand in front of their face, but I thought they were exaggerating. Now I knew they weren't.

I could not see where I was going, every direction looked the same, and everything was white! Normally, there was no way I could get lost up there; it didn't matter which direction you went, after walking for fifteen minutes you would either come across a road, stream, or someone's house. But I knew I had better go home, so I turned around and started back. My tracks were already covered up, but I was sure I knew which way to go. I walked and walked but I realized didn't know where I was. Now I didn't know which way to

45

go. I just started walking in what I thought was a straight line, but after thirty minutes I still was up on the hill. I should have come out of the woods by now.

I was lost and wasn't sure what I should do. I did have my matches and I started to gather small twigs to start a fire. If I was going to have to spend any length of time out here, I would have to stay warm. It wasn't long after I got the fire started that the wind died down and the snowstorm started to pass. I could see that I was almost in the same place as when the storm had started. I heard that when people were lost, they would walk in circles; now I knew it was true. I put out the fire and headed home.

"Where were you during that storm?" asked my mother.

Oh no, did she know I was lost? "Oh, I was up in the woods, I made a fire and waited it out."

"You should have come home, not stayed up in the woods."

"It was snowing so hard you couldn't tell one direction from the other, so I just stayed put and built a fire."

"I guess that was the smart thing to do. At least you got home before supper. You know how mad your father gets when you're late."

Boy, did I ever. That was like the 'cardinal sin'. No matter what I did, "don't be late for supper!" I had hoped to get a Hopalong Cassidy watch like Tubby had for Christmas, but I didn't get it. All I got was clothes. Clothes are NOT a good present for a kid. Unless it is a pair of those winter boots with the felt lining - now that would be a good clothes present. Or a pair of sheepskin mittens with a removable lining. Things like that I could use when I made my move to Canada! I did get the mittens one year, and I still have them, but I could always use another pair.

A few days later Tubby and I were going up the hill and we passed Andy's house. It was a big white three story Victorian house with an attic above. His father was a boss in the mill and he didn't normally hang around with us. Not because he thought he was better than us, but because his father used to take him places like the real ski slopes, where you would pay to ski. They had a big black Lincoln and his father kept his "white hat" from the mill, with his name on it, on the rear window deck. I think his father wanted everyone to know that he was a boss in the mill. Although, once, he did ask me to go swimming at the Country Club they belonged to, but I didn't want to go. I don't really care for swimming, not after what had happened at Fichtner's.

Andy was coming out of his house with the oddest pair of skis I ever saw. They were very narrow and had a strange binding on them.

"Hey you guys, want to go cross-country skiing with me?" asked Andy.

"We don't have cross-country skis," answered Tubby.

"My brothers aren't using theirs and I think we have some boots that will fit you. Come on and give it a try."

"Ok, I'd like to try it!" I replied. This would be another useful skill for Canada. We went into his basement and there were bikes and skis of every different size and style, it was like going into a sporting goods store. I never saw so much athletic equipment. Andy did have a big family; I never knew exactly how many brothers he had. I don't think there were any girls, other than his mother, in the family.

After trying on a few pairs of boots, Tubby and I finally found some that would fit us. We then set off to the old Clackum farm that hadn't been used for years. The family had died off years ago and there was no one that wanted to take the place over; it had been neglected for years. The farmhouse was falling down and the old barn had caved in years ago. The silo and corncrib were slowly leaning to one side, and it was only a matter of time until they also fell over. We went through the break in the tree line and we could see the remains of the fence that had kept the cows from wandering off. There was only a few hundred feet of fence still standing.

Andy explained to us how to do cross-country skiing. It was mostly done on level land with a few gentle slopes going downhill. Then, when you had to go up hill, you kept your skis on and went up diagonally. This seemed like too much work for me. I would sooner go downhill skiing. After a few hours of this, I was ready to call it a day. Tubby had been complaining the whole time. I didn't get an argument from him. We went back to Andy's house and put the skis away.

We thanked Andy and he said he wanted to do it again tomorrow. We both told him we couldn't make it. I said, "We're going to make an igloo in my yard. Want to join us?"

"Yeah, that would be great. What time?" asked Andy.

47

"After lunch."

"Ok, I'll see you then." Andy then went back inside and closed the door.

"What igloo?" asked Tubby.

"With all this snow we've had, there's a big pile in my yard from my father shoveling it off the roof. He was afraid it would cave in from the weight."

"And, how do you make an igloo? Aren't they made of ice blocks?"

"They might be at the North Pole, but all we have to do is hollow out this big pile of snow with shovels."

"You make everything sound simple, but it never is."

"Just be at my house tomorrow with a pointed shovel, not a snow shovel, and I'll show you!"

"Ok, I'll be there. I have to see this."

The next day, after lunch, Tubby and Andy showed up. The pile of snow was about eight feet high and ten feet square. I marked an area on one side where the entry would be and told them just to start removing snow from there and throw it on top of the pile. With the three of us working, it didn't take too long, to start to see a dark empty cavern appear in the pile.

Tubby didn't think it was going to work, and he was actually amazed. Andy, on the other hand, thought I did this all the time and knew it would work.

We ended up with the largest igloo I ever saw. "Thanks guys! I couldn't have done this without you!" I told them.

"You're darn right about that," yelled Tubby.

"Now what happens?" asked Andy.

"That area we didn't remove in the back is where we will sit," I told him.

"You mean, you just go in there and sit?" asked Tubby.

"Yeah, what did you think we were going to do with it?" I asked.

"I never gave it much thought, or I probably would have stayed home and watched Disneyland on TV!" replied Tubby. "Come on Andy, let's go to my house and watch TV."

"Hey, don't you at least want to go in and try it out?" I asked them as they trotted off toward Tubby's house.

"No, but you can come and watch TV if you want!"

So much for the igloo. It seemed like a good idea at the time. Now it was just a big pile of hollow snow, sitting in my backyard. It was too cold inside to be of any use. That was my first and last igloo. My father wasn't too happy in April when that pile of snow was still there. But it finally did melt.

A few days later, my father told us we were going for a Sunday drive. We hadn't been on a Sunday drive since October when the sky was bright blue and the leaves were yellow and crimson. I asked where we were going and he said that since I liked skiing so much, we were going to go to the ski slope and watch them ski. I had never been to a real ski slope, just the hills around here. I knew we were only going to watch, but this still would be great.

We piled into the car and headed out of town and up over the mountain past Dunnies, Luthers and Pickin' Chicken restaurant toward Ligonier. We got about half way down the mountain and came upon a truck pulling a trailer filled with hay. It was only going about 25 miles an hour in a 50 mile an hour zone.

"Oh fiddlesticks!" yelled my father. "Don't tell me we are going to have to follow this guy the whole way to Ligonier."

We finally got to the bottom of the mountain and the road leveled out and my father was about to pass the truck, but there was a car coming in the opposite direction. "Fiddlesticks!"

A few miles later the truck made a left turn on to a side road, "Finally, now we can make some time," said my father, relieved that the truck was gone.

We got to Ligonier and went around the "Diamond" as they call it, even though it is a square. We went past the old Fort Ligonier Hotel that burned down a few years later. We had been on a Sunday drive and parked the car along the street leading into the "Diamond." As we walked toward the square my mother said, "I smell smoke, don't you?"

"Now that you mention it, I do," replied my father.

We got to the square and as we turned toward the hotel, we could see the hole in the landscape where the hotel once stood. The only remnants were a pile of burnt wood and smoldering ashes with a putrid, sour smell. As we walked past the smoking pile, a gentleman emerged from the other side of the pile in a butler's uniform. He came staggering toward us and, slurring his words in a thick English accent, sobbed, "What am I going to do now? My hotel has burned down. I was the doorman there. I have nowhere to stay or work. There are no other hotels around that meet my standards. I will have to go back to England."

He didn't wait for an answer, he just stumbled off, down the sidewalk, weaving from side to side. Apparently he was drowning his sorrows with alcohol that was in the brown paper bag he was carrying.

We went out the other side of the square past the fort and onto route 30, the Lincoln Highway. Now we could make some time. We were going past the Rolling Rock Hunt Club, founded by the Mellon family, when up ahead, the truck pulling the trailer filled with the hay pulled out onto the highway in front of us!

"Fiddlesticks! I don't believe it. It's impossible - how could he get here ahead of us. It can't be the same truck," my father went on and on.

"I guess he knows a shortcut," said my mother. "It's the same truck. I remember that sign on the back. It says Nature Farms, Ryot, Penn."

"What! Not Joe Nature, it can't be. We will be following him the whole way up the mountain then if he is going to Ryot."

We did follow him the whole way up the mountain. My father apparently accepted this fact, since there were only a few "Fiddlesticks!" and "Poppycocks!" said on the way up the mountain.

We turned off the highway and onto the narrow road leading to the ski slope. Luckily the truck did not make the turnoff. We were about a half-mile from the entrance when all of the traffic came to a halt. "Oh fiddlesticks!" my father muttered. "I wonder what the hold up is?"

Then we started creeping along. About fifteen minutes later we arrived at the entrance. We pulled up to the entrance and the attendant told my father, "Five dollars please."

"Five dollars for what?" he asked.

"To go into the park."

"Oh, we don't want to ski, we just want to watch."

"Like I said, five dollars."

50

"Blimey, I'm not paying five dollars to watch."

"Then just pull through and turn back and go out the other gate."

With that my dad started to go. The car jerked to a stop and died. He tried starting it a few times, but it just groaned and would not even try to start.

"Could you push us off to the side?" my father asked the attendant.

"No, push it yourself; though, I will call maintenance to see if they can help you get it started."

"Can you believe that?" my father asked my mother. "Bloody hell, I can't believe he wouldn't push us off to the side! What's this world coming too?"

"Well, at least he is calling someone to help," replied my mother.

"I still can't believe that he wouldn't push us."

My father was more concerned that the guy wouldn't give us a push and he had to do it himself than he was with the car not running. My mother steered the car and my father and I pushed it to the side. About ten minutes later an old beat up Jeep came along with a guy in overalls. He had a pair of jumper cables and he told my father to open the hood, and he hooked up the cables and gave us a jump. Luckily it started.

"If I were you, I would stop at the first garage and get a new battery. Don't let it stall before then, and don't turn it off or you'll need another jump," he told my father.

"Right oh!"

He just looked at my father as if he was from another planet. "Now that guy knows how to treat people," my father told my mother.

That was the first and last time I got to go to a real ski slope. I must say, the snow was sure deep up there, and it would be there until May! Almost like Canada. We did make it to a garage and my father got a new battery. Then all he did was complain about the cost. First the guy wouldn't give us a push and now the price of a battery has gone sky high, "What's the world coming too?" he muttered.

February was coming to an end, we had a snowstorm and the weather was warm. It was one of those snows that are wet and great for making snowmen. I ran to Tubby's house and told him I had an idea to make a giant snowball.

"Not another of your great ideas. I don't think I can take anymore of them," said Tubby.

"All we have to do is go to the old Clackum farm and up to the that big field on the hill. We start rolling a snowball across the top and when it gets too big to push, we push it down the hill and it will roll by itself, creating the biggest snowball anyone has ever seen."

"You know, that might be a good idea, and it doesn't sound like too much work; not like the igloo idea. That was just crazy - my arms are still sore," replied Tubby.

We headed up to the old farm where we had gone cross-country skiing with Andy. We started rolling a snowball. As we rolled it, it would pick up all the snow right down to the grass. It looked more like a giant cinnamon roll than a snowball. In between the layers of white snow were dark layers of dirt, dried leaves, and grass, instead of cinnamon. We looked back and there was a bare path in the snow following behind us. It didn't take too long for it to be so big and heavy we couldn't push it anymore. We both tried pushing it toward the steep slope. It took all we had to get it to move a few inches.

"We need more help," said Tubby.

"Hey, there's Andy and his brothers, cross-country skiing. Andy!! Up here!" I yelled.

The three of them saw us and came up the hill to see what was going on.

"What the heck are you guys doing?" asked Andy.

"We're trying to make the worlds biggest snowball, but we can't roll it any further. We want to get it over to the hill and let it roll down," I told him.

"We can try and help push it." The five of us started to push and slowly the huge ball started to move.

One of the brothers hollered, "Keep pushing! Don't stop or we'll never get it going again."

We had the giant snowball about three feet from the edge of the hill and it stopped and we could not get it moving again.

"We're going to need more help," I said.

"Either that or just let the thing here, it's not going to go anywhere," said Andy. With that Andy and his brothers left. They said they were sorry they couldn't help, but they had to get home.

"What we need is a lever," said Tubby.

"A what?" I asked him.

"A lever, a long piece of wood or an iron bar. Something to put under this ball and give it a good push. We're almost to the edge of the hill, it won't take much to get it over there."

I couldn't believe Tubby was more enthusiastic about this than I was. It was usually the other way around.

"Let's go to the dump and see if we can find something we can use to push it," I told him, and off to the dump we went. And whom should we run into? Joe, of all people. Something bad was going to happen, I just knew it.

"Where are you guys going?" he asked. We told him what we were doing. He said that his father once had an old boat oar made of oak and if he could find it, we could try and use that.

We went to Joe's house and into the garage. There, sitting in the middle of the garage, was an old beat up Chevy with big fat fenders. They didn't make them like that anymore. Joe told us it was his fathers and his mother didn't drive, so it just sat there and hadn't moved since his father died. It was covered in dust, with dents, and it had scratches of many colors all over.

Joe was looking up at the rafters in the garage. He was sure that was the last place he had seen the oar.

"There it is," he shouted. He got an old wooden stepladder from the corner of the garage and placed it under the oar and climbed up and retrieved it.

It was a long oar and after Joe wiped the dust off, it revealed a very shiny, lacquered finish. I had no idea what kind of boat this was used on. It seemed too big for a canoe. It was a work of art. We headed back to the Clackum place to finish making the big snowball.

When we got there, Joe could not believe the size of the snowball. He saw the path we had made in the snow and asked how we were able to push it that far. We told him about the help we got from Andy and his brothers.

"If the five of you couldn't push it any further, how do you think the three of us can move it?" asked Joe.

"That's why we need the oar," replied Tubby. "We have to use it as a lever, put it under the ball and pull up on the oar and inch it over to the edge of the hill. We are only a few feet away from it now."

We forced the oar under the big ball and we all got under the oar and pushed up on the end of it. It slowly moved a few inches and it made groaning noises as it moved. We did this several times, readjusting the oar each time. Then with one last push, the giant ball reached the edge of the hill and started rolling on its own. The oar was stuck in the big ball and it kept moving with it, and so did Joe!

"Let go of the oar!!" Tubby and I both hollered, but Joe seemed to just hang on to that oar. Both Joe and the oar disappeared over the top as the big ball started slowly rolling down the hill. It started going faster and faster. Then all of a sudden we saw Joe fly off to the side as the ball picked up even more speed and flew down the hill and across a small stream. Then as it went up the slope toward the road, it began to lose momentum. I kept hoping that it would stop before it got to the road.

The big ball started to slow down as it approached the road and I thought that it was going to go out onto the road and smash into a car. But, it stopped a few feet before the road. That big ball was there until the end of May. Everyone wondered what it was and how it got there. No one ever said it was Tubby and I.

"Joe, why didn't you let go of that oar?" I asked him. "You almost got smashed!"

"My sleeve got caught on the end of the oar and I couldn't get it off until I started going over the top. Believe me, I wanted to let go, I thought I was going to get squashed!"

We didn't find Joe's oar until the big ball started melting in May. If Joe hadn't got off, we might not have found him until then either! That was the end of February, winter was coming to an end. I was sad to see it go. Hopefully we would get one or two more snows in March. I would have to wait and see.

Chapter 5

It was now March and all of the snow was practically gone except for a small patch on the north side of the cemetery where it was in the shade most of the day. There was a small hill about fifty feet long with a few inches of slush still on it. I would spend all day sled riding down this hill and pulling my sled back up again. I was the only one there and I was happy. Everyone else was riding bicycles or shooting hoops at the playground. I would rather be doing this.

The next day even this small patch of snow had melted. It was a warm, windy day and I went to the West End General Store and bought a kite and a ball of string for fifteen cents. I went home and put the kite together and found some old material my mother had in the ragbag to make a tail.

I then went to the graveyard - where else would you go to fly a kite? I wasn't there too long when Ricky, one of the younger neighborhood kids, showed up with a kite too. He wanted to have a battle with our kites, but I told him if we did that, only one of us would be left with a kite, the other would just blow away in the wind after the string was cut. He said he didn't realize that and he didn't want to loose his kite. Me either, I just paid ten cents for it.

I had my kite out on all 500 feet of string. Ricky was not having any luck getting his kite up, so I asked him if he would watch my kite and give the string a few tugs when it started to drift down. He agreed and then I ran over to the little store and bought another spool of string for a nickel. I almost blew my whole weeks allowance of twenty-five cents in one day. I ran back with my string and tied it onto the end of the first spool and started giving the kite more string.

I told Ricky how to get his kite up in the air as I was giving my kite more string. He ran along with his kite over his head and started giving it a little string at a time. It wasn't long before he had his kite about 100 feet up in the air. My kite was almost up to 1000 feet in the air, when all of a sudden the string broke and my kite started lazily swaying from side to side and slowly descended into the trees up on the hill. I tried to figure out about where the kite came down, about halfway along the hillside, somewhere between the first and second road.

I wound up the remaining string, which was about a spool and a half, and told Ricky I was going to find my kite and wished him luck. I headed up the hill to where I thought the kite came down. I couldn't see it anywhere. It was like looking for a needle in a haystack. There were no leaves on the trees yet, and I thought the brightly colored kite would stand out against the drab color of the trees. I zigzagged across that hillside all evening and the next day. I never did find it. So much for kite season. I only bought one kite a year and it always ended up in a tree somewhere. In the fall after the leaves fell off, I would see the skeleton of my kite. Almost all the colorful paper would be gone. Just the wooden frame and tail would be left hanging in the tree. A reminder of all the fun I had flying it.

A few days latter I saw Tubby over in the graveyard with what appeared to be a large cross in his hands. I couldn't imagine what he was trying to do. I ran down to see what was going on. As I got closer I could see that he had the largest kite I had ever seen. It was as big as Tubby and was made of clear plastic with a heavy wooden frame and a large tail hanging from it.

"Tubby, where did you get that giant kite?" I asked him.

"Oh, hi Dandy. My old man made it for me. They had a piece of equipment delivered to the mill wrapped in heavy plastic and they were just going to throw it into the furnace, so he asked if he could have it. You know him, he won't let anything go to waste. Then he got the idea to make a kite."

"That thing sure is huge. How is it to fly?"

"I don't know, I haven't been able to get it off the ground yet. I think it will have to be a very windy day before it will take off."

Just then the wind did start to pick up. It blew the baseball cap off of my head. I ran after my hat. Tubby held the kite over his head and started running down the hill while I held onto the string and ran after him. After a few tries, the kite did start to go up in the air, but it would not stay up. It would go up and then start to make a clockwise loop and then come straight down and bury the front of the kite into the ground. When it did finally take off, the string broke and the kite came straight down like a rocket. We both ran out of the way so we didn't get hit or it would have done some serious damage to us.

"I think you need to get a heavier string for this kite," I told Tubby.

"Yeah, I guess so. But if the string is heavier I don't think the kite will stay up in the air, it will be too heavy."

"Don't use a rope, just some heavier string or even better, some fishing line. Yeah, I bet that would work."

"I'll take this home and see if my old man has some heavier string or fishing line. But I won't be back today; I'm getting tired of running down the hill and dragging this thing back up. Maybe I'll see you tomorrow."

"OK, I'll look to see if I have some heavy fishing line at home, too. I'll let you know if I find any. See you tomorrow," I told him as I turned to go home.

Then next day we had a heavy snowfall and I forgot about the kite and got my sled out and went sled ridding. No one else came over to the graveyard; I couldn't believe I was the only one out. Everyone else must have been tired of sled riding. Not me; I just kept sledding down the hill and walking back up, all day long.

I was looking forward to the next day to go sledding again. But after eating my Puffed Rice, I saw that it started to rain. There is nothing worse than rain. It soaks you to the bone and makes you feel miserable. You can't go outside and play if it is raining. You can't do anything without an umbrella.

So I broke into my piggy bank and took out my life savings. I put on my big rubber boots, got an umbrella, and I walked down the brick road into the city. The fog was thick from the cold snow and warm air. It was a very dismal day with the warm wind blowing in my face. The water from the melting snow was running down the street like a small stream. As I crossed the road to the other side, the water kept running into my boots and flying up in the air and I had to face my umbrella into the spray to keep dry. I would jump off the road when a car came by, otherwise I would have been drenched from the slush and water being thrown up by the car.

I went to the West End General Store. This was one of my favorite stores. They had everything you could ever want. From puzzles and toys to carbide cannons and Ouija Boards, they had it all. I once bought a kaleidoscope that had various colored crystals inside that made different patterns as the front was turned. I spent many hours looking through it at all the different designs.

I bought a model of an Eskimo on a dog sled. This was the only model they had that reminded me of winter in the great north woods. It only cost seventy-five cents, so I didn't have to spend all of my money.

I worked all day on it. It was a very good way of passing the time on a rainy day with the snow melting away outside. After this I watched Sergeant Preston on TV. Hopefully tomorrow would be better. I hoped for snow, but I doubted if it would come. That was one thing about March - it could be seventy degrees with a warm wind blowing one day and thirty with blowing snow the next.

Tubby never did get that kite to fly, it was just too big. I guess that is why they are made of paper and light balsa wood. His father told him it needed a longer tail and with all that weight it would never get off the ground. He used the plastic to cover his pile of firewood.

After this, his father got Tubby's old steel tricycle, since he was too big to ride it, and took off the seat and handlebars, and turned the frame upside down. He then put the handlebars back on. It was the oddest thing I had ever seen. Then he placed padding on the back step and that is where Tubby would sit. With the low center of gravity, it would not tip over. Tubby could go twenty miles an hour down through the graveyard with no problem.

We spent many days taking this thing to all sorts of places to see how fast we could go on it. We even tried taking it down the brick road, but we quickly found out that without any brakes, that was not a smart thing to do. Tubby was going too fast to make the sharp turn at Hudson's and went right through her flowerbed. Many years later the Marx Company came out with the Big Wheel Tricycle; it looked just like the thing Tubby's father had made, only theirs was plastic. He was a man ahead of his time!

58

Chapter 6

March turned into April, April into May and before you knew it, it was summertime, dreaded summertime. I didn't like the heat, I didn't like swimming, I didn't like the bugs or anything about summer except that we didn't have to go to school. That was the only good thing about summer.

With all the time we had on our hands, we could go up the hill to the woods and build a cabin. Every year we would build at least one cabin. Sometimes it would be a tree house up in the trees, or else a lean-to or a log cabin on the ground. It was different every time. I did like this part of summer. It was cool in the woods. We would stay up there all day working on the cabin. I can't ever remember going home for lunch during these times. Then when it was done, we would sit inside and look out at the birds and animals that came by.

Some nights we would sleep out in the cabin. We would bring beans, bacon, eggs and something to drink. We would make a fire to cook and keep warm in the evenings. It was a fun time. Then one night when Tubby, Andy and I were sleeping out, we were awakened by the sound of someone chopping wood off in the distance.

I was the first one to wake up, then Andy, and then Tubby.

"What the heck is that?" asked Andy.

"It sounds like someone chopping wood," I replied.

"What time is it?" asked Tubby.

"You're the one with the Hopalong Cassidy watch, you tell me," I replied.

"It's one in the morning," answered Tubby groggily.

"Come on, lets go see who it is," said Andy.

We went off in the direction of the chopping, along the ridge and down the hill toward Stump Creek. As we walked along in the dark, it seemed that we were not getting any closer to the sounds. It always seemed to be about 100 yards away. It was a steady chopping sound that would go on for a few minutes, then stop for a few minutes. This just kept repeating over and over. Then the chopping stopped.

"I don't know about you guys, but this is giving me the creeps," whispered Tubby.

"Yeah, I know what you mean. I don't like it either," whispered Andy.

"Why are.." I started

"Keep your voice down," whispered Tubby.

"Why are we whispering?" I asked.

"Because this is spooky and I don't know who is doing this, but obviously he knows we are following him, because he keeps moving away. That's why," whispered Tubby.

"Now you guys are making me nervous," I said in a hushed voice. "I am going back to the cabin."

"Yeah, that sounds like a good idea," whispered Andy.

With that we all headed back to the cabin. The next day we met at the playground. Andy was there with a few of his brothers. We started talking about the "wood chopper" and Andy's brother said he also had heard the "wood chopper" when he slept out over the years.

"You mean he has been up there for years?" I asked.

"Oh yeah! He won't hurt you. You will never find him, he just keeps moving away," said Andy's older brother.

We could not get the woodchopper out of our minds. That night Tubby and I went back up to the cabin and we were not there very long before the chopping started. We started walking toward the sounds and again it kept the same distance away from us.

"I have an idea," said Tubby. "Let's start walking the other way, away from the sounds, and see what happens."

"Hey, that is a good idea," I replied.

We turned around and started walking back to the cabin. The sounds started coming toward us. Now I was beginning to think that this was not such a great idea after all. Now he was following us and this was giving me the creeps.

"Tubby, this is starting to give me goose bumps."

"Dandy, you're never happy, are you?"

"I would be happy if the guy would just go away."

All of a sudden there was a loud scream like a baby crying. It sounded like it came from just over the hill in front of us. Now we had the woodchopper coming up behind us and a baby screaming in front of us.

"Jesus, Tubby, what was that?"

"I don't know, but now I'm getting goose bumps. I knew we should have brought our BB guns."

"I'm not sure if that would help. What are we going to do now?"

"Let's start running to our left, up to campsite, then over to the green houses. Then we can take the road back home."

So off we ran as fast as we could, up to campsite where there was a large old crab apple tree that hung over the path. There was a fire pit made of fieldstone where people would come and cook out. Just our luck, there was no one there. We kept running past the greenhouses, where the full moon was reflecting off the glass and made them look like a lake through the trees, then out onto the road. This was the longer way home, but it was the safest.

We couldn't hear the woodchopper or the baby crying. We slowed down to a trot then, as we were both out of breath, and we started walking as we got closer to home.

"No one is going to believe us when we tell them what happened," said Tubby.

"The woodchopper was bad enough, but that baby crying did it for me. I don't think I am going back up there after dark anymore," I said with a quivering voice.

"There has to be a logical explanation for all of this. My old man will know what it is."

"I don't think your dad can explain a baby crying in the woods. This is something supernatural, like in the movies."

"Well, when I get home, I am going to tell him all about this...."

Just then, as we were passing the Indian Caves, there was a hair-curling scream, like a baby, coming from the caves. We both took off running for home and did not stop until we got there.

"That's it!" I exclaimed. "I am never going into the woods at night again. No more sleeping out for me. You couldn't drag me up there in the dark!"

"Yeah, I don't think I'll be going up there for a while either."

"For a while?? I'm never going back there in the dark again. And how did that baby get to the Indian Caves so fast? That's what I want to know."

"It couldn't have been the same baby."

"You mean that there is a group of babies up there waiting to scare the crap out of us?"

"I told you there has to be a logical explanation for this. Let's go over to the playground and see if anyone is there."

"Yeah, I don't want to go home yet. I need time to calm down first. If my mom saw me like this, she would never let me out of the house again."

Off we went to the playground. There sitting on the front steps were Andy and his older brother. We told them about our adventure and Andy could not believe we heard a baby crying in the woods or at the Indian Caves. Although his older brother had heard about this and told us that years ago a car with a family was coming down the road one winter night and skidded on the ice and went over the edge into the Indian Caves and a baby in the car was killed. He said that on clear nights with a full moon you could sometimes hear a baby crying in the caves.

I was getting goose bumps and the hair on the back of my neck was standing up. This was not calming me down. I now was wishing that I had gone home instead of coming here. But that didn't explain the baby crying in the woods and Andy's brother had never heard of a baby crying out in the woods - that was a new one.

The next day I met Tubby over at the playground. He said his father heard the story about the car crashing at the Indian caves, but it was only cats that hang out there, and when they cry, they sound like a baby crying. The baby in the woods was probably a Fisher Cat. Or it may have been a rabbit in distress; they make a noise that sounds like a baby crying.

"Your father sure knows a lot of stuff," I told Tubby.

"Yeah, he reads a lot. He said there never was a car that crashed into the caves; someone made that up."

"But what about the woodchopper; how did he explain that?"

62

"He said it's some guy that sells firewood, and he travels all over the place cutting up trees that have fallen down. He also said that the sounds travel down through the valleys and it sounds like he is just up ahead, and when you go toward the sound it seems to move away. Something to do with acoustics, he said."

"Boy, I hope he is right. So we should just ignore the woodchopper and not worry about the crying babies?"

"That's what he says. If we don't, our imaginations will run wild."

It was another hot summer day, and I had saved up my allowance since we had been up in the woods for the past few weeks. There was nowhere to spend money up there. I was going to Silver's Drug Store to get a Cherry Smash. I took a shortcut down the "snake bug trail" where the blackberry and elderberry bushes grew tall and formed an arch overhead. It was filled with spider webs and the occasional snake. I then ran down the street and through the alley. Then I heard what sounded like some one yelling "Raah an booone, Raaah an boone," over and over.

As I walked further along, down to an intersecting street, I saw a cart with pots and pans swinging back and forth, hanging on the sides, pulled by a sway back horse with a straw hat on his head and his ears sticking through the brim. It was Old Joe the Rag and Bone Man.

"Raaaag an Boooone," he yelled as he slowly made his way along the back streets and alleys of the neighborhoods. Women would come out with old pots and pans, rags, or bones. In return, he would give them clothes pins, or pegs as he called them, or a peg bag if the item given to him was worth more.

"Raaaag an Booooone," he repeated over and over. I would always pet the horse when I ran into them. Joe was an elderly gentleman with patched up overalls, a white beard, and a straw hat to match the one his horse wore. I never did find out the name of the horse. He looked old and was brown with white markings. He had a long white tail and mane, and big brown eyes with long eyelashes.

There were pots and pans hanging from the sides of the cart, bones and rags piled up in the back of the wagon behind the seat. There was a swarm of flies flying around the bones and the

63

wagon in general. The horse kept swishing his tail and his skin kept twitching to chase the flies away.

I liked horses, but these flies were starting to come after me, so I trotted off down the alley to Silver's Drug Store. It was nice and cool inside and I was the only customer there. Since the Dairy Dell opened up the street, not as many people came in for soda fountain drinks, just to get prescriptions filled. They preferred the more modern Dairy Dell. It was now the place to hang out and meet your friends. There was brighter fluorescent lighting at the Dairy Dell, but I liked the darker incandescent lighting here better; it gave the place a melancholy atmosphere, the same as the Marigold Restaurant up the street. It looked like something out of the movie the "Maltese Falcon."

I ordered a Cherry Smash and put my nickel on the counter. The waitress returned with my drink and took my money. She went over to a big brown cash register and punched a key. A big white square popped up in the clear window above the keys with a black five on it and the drawer flew out at the same instant with the sounds of the coins banging around inside.

I finished my drink and went outside into the hot air. I now wished I had brought my bike; I could be home in five minutes if I had. Now it would take at least twenty minutes to walk home. I went past Putt's Tire and Battery and looked in the window. There was the Stewart Warner bicycle speedometer, still in the window. I was trying to save up my money to buy it, but at $5.95 it was going to take a lot of odd jobs. Tubby and I did try selling clothes props. We went up into the woods and cut down saplings and sold them for twenty-five cents each or five for a dollar. But we only sold five. We had to split the dollar, so we each made fifty cents on that venture. Then the lady complained because they were so heavy. We tried to explain that since they were just cut down, the sap was in them and after a while they would dry out and be light. She seemed satisfied with that and we left as fast as we could before she changed her mind.

Our next idea was to caddy at the local country club. It seemed like a good idea, $2.25 to carry a golf bag around the course for 3 hours, or $5.00 to carry two bags. I though I should start out with just one bag and see how that would go. I am glad I did. Just my luck I got some guy with a kangaroo bag. It had more and bigger pouches than a kangaroo. It must have weighed 30 pounds. He had his lunch and two bottles of whiskey, which he shared with his buddy, four big wooden drivers, five assorted putters, nine iron clubs, and three-dozen balls. By the time we were done, he only had about one half dozen left. He was in the woods looking for his ball most of the time and he hit every water hazard that they had. My shoulder was so sore after that, I didn't go back for two weeks.

That was the hardest I ever worked for $2.25, although he did give me a twenty-five cent tip and bought me a Coke and pack of crackers at the ninth hole snack shack. Then we had to walk back home, about a three-mile walk through Stackhouse Park and up through the Guinea field. Of course Tubby wanted to stop at a store to get something to eat and drink. He would spend half of his earnings on food. Not me, I was saving every penny I made to get that speedometer. I didn't care about the speed, it was the mileage that I wanted to keep track of. I wanted to see how far I traveled on my Raleigh 3-speed English racing bike. I did go back several times after that, but it turned me off golfing for the rest of my life. I never had any desire to go golfing and chase that little white ball around the golf course.

That summer, I helped my grandfather build a small plank house on his property. He would rent it out once it was completed. I held boards while he cut them. I mixed cement, or mud, as he called it. I carried boards, shingles, and siding. I ran to the hardware store to get nails, but I had to make sure that I mentioned it was for my grandfather so he would get his twenty-five percent discount. He paid me one dollar a week; we worked all week and half a day on Saturday - that was payday. Although, every evening when we were done working for the day, he would usually give me a dime or a quarter and say, "Here, stop at the little store, and get a candy bar and a Coke on your way home," as he reached into his bib overalls and pulled out a hand full of change.

By the end of summer I had enough money to buy the speedometer. I went to Putt's on Saturday morning and purchased it. The total price was $6.19 with tax. That was the biggest purchase I had ever made. I pedaled home as fast as I could so I could install it on the front wheel. It was not too difficult to install, I just had to remove the front wheel and place the round disk on the axle with the bump out between the spokes, and then replace the wheel. I then removed the bolt from the gooseneck, placed the speedometer on the bracket, and put the bolt through and replaced the bolt. As my father used to say, "Bob's your uncle!" I was done.

I rushed over to the playground and did a few laps. I got it up to 15 miles an hour and after 4 laps I only had 4 tenths of a mile. Only 4 tenths? How far was I going to have to go to get a mile? I started to ignore the mileage and just checked it every half hour or so. The miles started adding up then. Then after a while I would only check it when I started out in the morning, and then once or twice during the day. Tubby and I used to average 20 miles a day on our bikes; he didn't know we went that far.

It was a cool August day and Tubby and I started riding our bikes. Tubby had a Schwinn Phantom bicycle with a big spring on the front. We went all over Johnstown, from Coopersdale to Ferndale and all the neighborhoods in between. As we were going through Roxbury, past the Bandshell, Tubby saw the custard stand near the miniature golf course. He could not pass this by. We went and stood in line to get our frozen custard. I just got a small one, but Tubby had to get the biggest one they had.

"This used to be a lake here," said Tubby pointing out at the baseball fields.

"What do you mean, a lake?" I asked him.

"Yeah, it was Luna Park. They had boats you could rent, and there were rides; it was an amusement park."

"How do you know all this stuff? It amazes me."

"Oh, my old man tells me about the old days."

"Boy, like I said before, your father sure knows a lot about everything."

"He reads a lot, too."

"Yeah, I know. You told me before."

We ate our cones and then took off down to Hornerstown and took a ride through Sandyvale Cemetery. Most of the tombstones were knocked over or washed away from the 1936 flood. The large stones, for the wealthy families, were still in place.

We then went over the Hickory Street Bridge to Kernville and rode past the big stately houses built at the end of the last century. Many of them still had the carriage houses out back; some had been converted into apartments.

We then went through downtown Johnstown past the Victorian style Carnegie Library. Andrew Carnegie had built 2209 libraries after the flood of 1889, one for each person killed in the flood. He had felt guilty because the South Fork Fishing & Hunting Club, where he was a member, had owned Lake Conemaugh and it broke and caused the flood. It was the largest man-made lake at that time.

We went through the Stone Bridge where all the debris from the flood collected during the flood, then caught fire and burned for days.

After we came out on the other side we went through Cambria City, past the old brewery and the mills in Lower Cambria. There was a smoke stack that had a blue flame burning at the top that was very vivid at night, but only barely visible during the day. It burned off the excess gas from the Coke Plants in the mill. We rode the back alley, where there was no traffic, and back to the West End, past the Harris and Boyer Bakery, where every Wednesday you could smell the bread baking all over town. They also made the famous Gobs there, and you could buy them in the day old shop in back at a reduced price. We finally made it back home to the playground and met Andy there.

"Hey Tubby, look, we have gone 25 miles already today," I said.

"Twenty five miles? It is only 1:00 Let's see how many miles we can go altogether today; maybe we can set a record," replied Tubby.

"I'm not doing anything today," said Andy, with disappointment in his voice. "My dad was called out to work this morning. Something happened to the furnace at his mill. We were going to go swimming, but I don't know when he will be back." He got on his bike and we started out on the next phase of our adventure.

We rode down the brick road and headed out the Haws Pike through the Conemaugh Gap. It is the deepest and steepest gorge east of the Rocky Mountains. It was a nice sunny day with a bright blue sky. The sign read "Seward 9 Mi." The road was fairly level as it followed the Conemaugh River through the gap. We went through Seward and over the bridge and through the railroad underpass. We then cut over to Cramer and came out at Joyland, the local bar in Cramer. We then took the Cramer Pike back to Johnstown. We had now gone through 4 counties so far today; that must have been a record in itself.

We got back to the Coopersdale section of Johnstown, past one of Haws Refractory plants with the beehive ovens where they baked the bricks. Haws and Swanks were the two major refractories in the area. There were others, but they were much smaller in size.

"I'm going to stop at Coes Subshop and get a pop. Anybody else want one?" asked Tubby.

"Are you buying?" I had asked him.

Tubby just laughed and said, "Yeah, right! You must be kidding, you know me better than that."

I sure did know better than that and I was just kidding. We were all thirsty after that ride, and we went in and each bought a bottle of pop.

"How many miles do we have now?" asked Andy.

"According to my speedometer, we have 47.6 miles so far. Well Tubby and I do. You didn't join us until we had already put on 25 miles."

"Well, if we break a record, I'll have to go 25 more miles after you are done. I want to be a part of this record setting thing."

"It may be too late in the day for you to do that, Andy. I am planning to go all day and see if I can make it to 100 miles tonight."

"Are you crazy!" asked Tubby. "I am ready to call it a day now!"

"We're almost half way there, now. Don't give up, we can do it."

"There is no way I am going to be able to go 100 miles today," said Andy. "I may as well go home now and see if my dad came home yet. I would sooner be swimming than doing this; it's getting too hot."

"You guys are a bunch of wimps. I am going to go 100 miles today."

"I want to see how many miles you have on that speedometer when I leave you today, then I want to see it again tomorrow morning, just to make sure you don't try to fool us," replied Tubby.

"Don't worry, I'll show you. Then you'll see that I did set a record."

"There's no way you can go 100 miles in one day. I don't think they go that far in the Tour de France in one day," exclaimed Tubby.

"Well I am going to do it. If you want to be a part of this, fine. If not, then too bad. I will go down in local history as "Dandy, the kid that bicycled 100 miles in one day." So you can do whatever you want."

"You think we will go down in history?" asked Andy.

"He doesn't know what he's talking about, Andy. Don't listen to him. Anyhow, you are already 25 miles behind."

"Well, I can't waste any more time here. I have to get home by five o'clock to eat and then I have a lot more miles to go," I told them as I got on my bike and started to pedal.

"Where are you going now?" asked Tubby.

"I think I will take a ride up to Hinkston Run Dam, past the Rosedale Coke Plant. Why, do you want to come along?"

"Yeah, I think I will, but then I am done and going home."

"I am going home. I'll see you guys tomorrow," said Andy.

We went back through Cambria City and crossed over the Ten Acre Bridge to Iron Street and then past Prosser Hollow to Minersville. We went past the gate to the Lower Works of Bethlehem Steel and up the hill overlooking the Rosedale Coke Plant. We could see the flames shooting out of the holes on top of the oven batteries as they were getting ready to push out an oven of coke. Then, further along the battery, we saw a worker with a long iron bar hit one of the five lids on the oven and it made a "pop" sound. He then pushed the lid away from the hole and moved on to the next and did the same for each one.

Then a worker in front of the oven came along on a funny looking contraption that moved to the front of the oven where the lids were taken off and he removed the door to the oven. It revealed a white-hot wall of coke. Then a big machine that ran on a track at ground level moved to the oven where the door was removed and lined up with the opening. A large iron piece, as big as the oven opening, started to push against the white-hot wall of coke.

The wind started to change directions and all of the smoke and the smell of the place started blowing our way. There was fine grit in the smoke and it stuck to our sweaty arms and faces. We both took off and headed for Hinkston Run Dam.

Once we got away from the Coke Plant we could hear the mourning doves' mournful cooing and the trees were hanging over the road. It was much cooler on the shady dirt road and it was filled with lots of potholes that we tried to avoid as we pedaled along. It was a gradual climb up to the dam; at least it would be downhill all the way back. We went along the dam and across the back and down the other side. There was a road that went over the spillway to the dam keepers house, but there was a "No Trespassing" sign, so we pedaled back the way we came. This would give us more miles anyway, as they were mounting up.

"Hey, Dandy, how many miles do we have now?" asked Tubby.

"We have exactly 82.9 miles. I think we will get 100 miles today," I told him.

"Well if you want to get home by 5:00, we better get moving. It's 4:10 now."

"Oh, you're right, we better get moving."

I pedaled as fast as I could; I didn't care if Tubby kept up or not. I had to be home by 5 o'clock. I don't know when I lost Tubby, but all I could think of was getting home. I retraced our route home and it was exactly 5:00 when I ran in the door.

"Just in time again, Daniel," my father stated. "Can't you be early just once?"

"I try to get here early every time, but it never works out that way," I told him.

"Fiddlesticks! If you tried to be early, then you would be early."

"Honest, I do try, but I just can't seem to get here early."

"Well, just don't be late. We all sit down together to eat."

I hurried up and ate everything on my plate.

"Can I be excused now?" I asked, to no one in particular.

"What's your hurry, we just sat down to eat," my father replied.

"I'm trying to set a record to see how may miles I can go on my bike in one day."

"You want to see if you can go, what, 20 miles in one day?" he asked.

"No, I want to see if I can go 100 miles in one day," I told him.

"Poppycock! You can't go 100 miles in a day," he said laughing.

"I already have 87 miles today."

"You have 87 miles today," he said in disbelief.

"Yes, I only need 13 more miles and I want to get going before it gets dark."

"How many times around the playground did you have to go to get 87 miles?" asked my mother.

"We were not on the playground, we went all over the place."

"Well you better be careful, there are a lot of cars on the road nowadays - more than when I was a kid. Back then you didn't have to worry about traffic like today. And watch out for the streetcar tracks, they can throw you over, don't I know it. That is how I got that scar on my arm," she said as she held up her arm to show me. She had told me this story dozens of times.

"I am very careful of the traffic and the streetcar tracks," I replied as I got up and ran out the door.

I went up to Tubby's house and called him. "Tuuubby! Tuuuuby!"

His mother came to the door and said, "Tubby told me to tell you he is not feeling very well and he won't be coming out tonight. He said he might see you tomorrow."

"Oh, ok. I hope it is not serious - he seemed ok earlier."

"I think he is just tired. He said you both have been riding bikes all day, and he is tired."

"Ok, I'll see him tomorrow."

I went down the street to the playground. I now had 88 miles, only 12 more to go. I didn't feel much like going down the hill to the city, I know how Tubby felt. So I just started riding around the playground, lap after lap. The more I looked at my speedometer, the harder it seemed. So I just kept pedaling, lap after lap, until it was dark.

I looked at my speedometer I had gone 99.7 miles, I only needed .3 more. I made a few more laps and I had 100.2 miles. I did it! I went 100 miles in one day. That record will stand forever!

The next day I went over to the playground and parked my bike. I had done enough pedaling to last me for a while. I sat on the steps in the shade under the tree. If Tubby wanted to see me, he was going to have to come and look for me. About an hour later I saw him come down the road and ride into the playground.

"Well, did you set a record?" he asked me.

"Look for yourself," I said pointing to my speedometer.

"Are you sure you did all these miles yesterday, or did you get up early and put them on today?" he asked.

"I'm too tired to do any biking today. I put them all on yesterday. After I called you, I came down here and kept riding around the playground until I got 100 miles."

"That must have been pretty boring."

"Yeah, it was, but I was determined to get to 100 miles since I was that close."

We never attempted to break that record and as far as I know, no one else tried to either. This was how our summer began. I was having fun, but I could not wait for winter to arrive. I did not like the heat. But the Fourth of July was just around the corner, or as my father called it "Guy Fawkes Day in America." This was another good thing about summer.

Chapter 7

The Fourth of July meant it was time to get out the carbide and find a can with a tight fitting lid. Every kid in the neighborhood was down at the dump looking for paint cans or any other type of can with a lid. There would also be a run on carbide at the local hardware store. The sales person never questioned why we were buying it or what it was being used for. Not like today, when you have to be 18 and show your ID to buy a can of spray paint. We were sure lucky back then, but we didn't know it. The world has changed a lot since then.

The year before I went all out and bought a two and half pound can of carbide, enough to last my entire childhood. I discovered that the can it came in made the best carbide-can you could find. The lid was very tight fitting and sealed in all the gasses and didn't let any escape. I would put several pieces of carbide in the can, then sprinkle some water from the pop bottle I had filled with water, replace the lid and hold my finger over the hole I had made in the bottom of the can, where the match would ignite the gas and a bright blue flame would shoot out of the hole and then blow the lid off with a BIG BOOM! That can was the envy of every kid in the neighborhood.

You could hear "boom, boom" coming from every section of the neighborhood. This would start around July first and continue until a few days after the fourth. As I look back, I am amazed that no one ever called the police. A few years later I traded that carbide can for a double bladed axe that I intended to take to Canada so I could build my log cabin. I still have the axe, but I am sure the can is now at the bottom of the dump rusting away.

After the Fourth of July, Tubby went on vacation to Atlantic City. His family went there every year. He would come back and tell me tales of how the under current almost pulled him out to sea, or a big wave came crashing down on him and he almost drowned. This made me glad that we never went to the ocean for a vacation.

I was riding my bike around the playground and I saw Joe come racing down the hill and standing on the seat of his bicycle!

"Joe! You're crazy, you know that," I hollered to him.

"Relax, Dandy, I know what I am doing. I have perfect balance," he told me.

"Yeah, until you fall and break a leg or something."

"Where is everybody?"

"Tubby is on vacation and Andy probably went swimming as usual. I don't know where everyone else has gone. It looks like it's just you and me. By the way, where have you been? I haven't seen you all summer."

"My old lady said she thought it would be good for me to go stay with my brother in Chicago for a while. So I have been out there until last night. I am glad to be back here. I could never live in the city, there is nothing to do there. I guess I missed all the fireworks over the Fourth?"

"Yeah, you did. It seemed as though there were more carbide cans this year than other years."

"My brother had M-80s and Cherry Bombs. They are legal out there, at least that is what he told me."

"The only thing legal here are sparklers and black magic snakes. Boring!"

"Yeah, it's a wonder they let us have carbide cans," said Joe sarcastically. "Let's go down to the Guinea Field and see what's going on there."

"Might as well, it's boring here. But lets try to stay out of trouble, and don't stand on your seat, ok?"

"Dandy, you're funny."

We got to the Guinea Field and it was empty - not a soul in sight. Usually someone was there hitting a ball or passing a football, but it was quiet. We rode over to the creek where it was shady and as we looked down the water it was all red!

"Hey, look!" yelled Joe. "They must be slaughtering up at the slaughterhouse. That's blood flowing in the water."

"You mean that the blood from the animals just goes into the creek?" I asked in amazement.

"Yeah, where did you think it went?"

"To tell the truth, I never thought about it."

"Come on, let's go up and watch. It'll be fun. Maybe we can get some cow horns."

"OK, I would like to get a cow horn. Maybe we could make a horn out of it."

"I did do that one year. You have to boil it to get the insides out."

"You mean they are not hollow? They're filled with something?" I asked.

"Yeah, you boil it, then beat it on a log or a stone and the inside slowly comes out clean as a whistle."

We arrived at the slaughterhouse and Joe rode around the side to the back where the cows were fenced in. He walked over to a door and opened it without hesitation. Against my better judgment, I followed. I was not prepared for what I saw. I really didn't know what to expect, but what I saw would haunt me for the rest of my life. I won't go into detail, but slaughtering animals is not a sight for the faint of heart. If you were not a vegetarian, you would be after witnessing this.

"Joe, I am going outside. I'll wait for you there," I told him.

"What's the matter, Dandy. Is this too much for you?" he asked me.

"Yes, it is. I don't like this. If you get a cow horn, see if you can get me one too."

"No, if you want one, stay here and get it yourself."

"No, I am going outside. See you there."

The smell of the place was beginning to make me sick, plus the sight I had just seen didn't help. It seemed like hours until Joe came out of the door with a large cow horn in each hand.

"Boy, you're nickname is fitting, you wimp. Here's your horn. I should have made you go in and get your own," he said as he threw the horn at me.

"Say what you like, but I don't like what I saw in there."

"They told me to tell you to come back on Monday. That's when they slaughter the pigs. Frank, the guy with one arm, said the pigs really squeal, and you would like that!"

"No thanks! I'll pass on that one."

We both had Raleigh bikes with a bag behind the seat, and we put the horns in our bags and rode home. Joe went to his house and got an old bucket and we went up the hill to the woods near the spring and filled the bucket with water. We then made a fire and boiled the horns for an hour or so. Then we beat them against a tree and sure enough the inside of the horn popped out, just like Joe said it would.

Needless to say, I never returned to the slaughterhouse to watch them slaughter any animals. Joe did explain how they slaughter the pigs and I am glad I never saw it. It is something worse than the way they slaughter the cows.

We returned to Joe's house and he got a hacksaw and cut the tip off the end of the horns. The he got a drill and dilled a small hole in the other end of the horns. Then he found some string and put it through the hole and tied it around the smaller end of the horn. Then he put the string over his shoulder with the horn against his back.

"This is how you carry the horn in the woods," Joe explained.

"Will this make any noise?" I asked him.

"Try it and see."

I blew through the horn, and to my amazement, it did make a noise like a horn.

"Now when we go up the hill, all we have to do is blow our horns to see if anyone is up there, instead of looking all over the place," I told him.

"Yep, that's all we have to do. Too bad no one else has one of these though. So it's only me and you, isn't that great?"

The more I thought about it, the more I didn't think it was so great. Just Joe and me? No way! I didn't need any trouble.

The following week Tubby came back from the shore and I told him about my experience at the slaughterhouse and making the cow horns. He thought it was hilarious, and asked why I didn't get him a horn.

"It's funny that you went there," said Tubby. "My father is going to butcher some of the older chickens today. I was going to ask if you wanted to come and help, but after what you just told me, I guess you don't want to come over."

"It can't be like slaughtering cows," I told him. "Sure, I'll come to watch; but I don't think I want to help."

"Ok, let's go to my place now. He will be starting soon."

As we got to Tubby's house I could see his father setting up a short fat log on end. It then looked like a tree stump sitting there. The chickens were in a fenced in area attached to the chicken coop. Most of the houses in the neighborhood had chicken coops, but not many were being used anymore. They were now used as storage sheds for tools and lawnmowers.

Tubby's father had a short handle hatchet that looked more like a tomahawk. He was sitting on the log with a file sharpening the hatchet. Back and forth the file would go, making the blade glisten in the sunlight.

"Ok, Tubby, go get that big rooster with the black tail feathers. We have had him forever," stated Tubby's dad.

Tubby opened the door to the fenced in area and the chickens all scattered as he walked in. The big rooster flapped his wings and flew a few feet and then landed and started running. Tubby ran after him and eventually caught him. He picked him up by his legs, and the bird was squawking and flapping his wings.

"Put him over here on the stump," his father yelled.

Tubby ran over and put the chicken's head and neck on the stump, and before I knew it the hatchet came down and the chicken's head rolled across the grass. Tubby let go of the big bird and it started running toward me!

I couldn't believe it. It was as if the thing could see me and was running right after me. I didn't cut its head off, it should be running after Tubby or his father. I took off running as fast as I could. I could hear Tubby and his father laughing, I didn't think it was funny at all. I just kept running and I didn't look behind me until I got home. Luckily the chicken was gone. I didn't know where it went, but I couldn't believe what I just experienced. Now I knew what they meant when they say "He was running around like a chicken with its head cut off."

This was twice in one week that I had seen animals being killed. Was someone trying to tell me something? I didn't like this summer at all. I couldn't wait for winter to get here.

I now had over 500 miles on my bike. I couldn't imagine that I had pedaled that much in such a short period of time. It was the end of July, the hottest part of summer. I pedaled up to the coal mine at the end of the street. It was always cool at the mine entrance. I heard that no matter what time of year it was, summer or winter, it was always 54 degrees inside the mine. I know it did feel cool here. The miners were not working now. Business was always slow at the end of summer. By September they would start working every day. The old mine pony, whose name was Bill, was in a fenced in area next to the mine entrance. Since they got the big electric motor to pull the mine cars out of the mine, they didn't need the pony anymore. The miners could not part with him and kept him around until he couldn't stand up any longer. Then they sold him to the glue factory.

Occasionally we would attempt to ride him, but he didn't like it. We would climb the apple tree and coax him over with apples, and then we would ease onto his back and hold on to his mane for dear life. He would rear up and start running around and kick his rear legs into the air. We would only last a minute or two and then be bucked off. At the time we thought this was fun, but as I look back I am amazed that we didn't get hurt.

I started walking into the mine. It was cool and damp with a musty smell and a trace of sulfur. There were small streams of water flowing on both sides of the tracks, and I walked on the mine ties to keep out of the water. I tried to avoid the large, greasy cable that ran down the center of the tracks that was used to pull the mine cars out. Every now and then I would step on the sheave wheels. I could hear a stone or something drop into the pooled water between the ties. It kept getting darker and darker. I could barely make out the mine posts, holding up the roof, along the walls. I kept walking until I saw that the entrance behind me looked like a small white dot. I then stopped. I did not want to go any further; it was getting spooky.

We all had been warned by our parents that we should not go into the mines in the area, but they were just too tempting. We never went in too far. The deepest we had ever gone was to the first branch. We were afraid we might get lost inside if there were more than one branch. We heard stories that the mine went under one of the cemeteries, and you could see the bottoms of the coffins in the roof of the mine. We did think that would be cool to see, but we never went in that far.

I turned around and started walking toward the pinpoint of light that was the entrance. It was nice and cool inside of the mine and I would have liked to stay there for a while, but it was just too creepy for me. If Tubby would have been with me I probably would have stayed there longer.

I emerged into the hot bright sunlight. It was so bright after being in the dark for so long that it hurt my eyes. The old mine pony was in the shade under the apple tree, munching away on apples. I went over and climbed up the tree and picked an apple and joined him. We both enjoyed the cool shade and the taste of the green apples. I could hear my mother saying "Don't eat too many of those green apples, you'll get sick.'

It was too late, I was addicted to them. There was nothing better than green apples with salt on them. I can never remember going home for lunch in those days. There were apple, pear, peach and cherry trees growing wild all over the hill. There were also plenty of blackberry, raspberry and elderberry bushes growing everywhere. Why would we go home to eat when everything was here? Then we would go over to the spring and get a drink of cold water. We had it made!

I then heard a twig snap and I looked over toward the path that came out of the woods and there was Scruffy, the village hermit, coming out into the open. He lived near the slaughterhouses in a tar-paper shack built into a rock outcrop on the side of the hill. I never knew it until years later after he died, and they tore the shack down, that it had a spring running through it. He had running water in that place.

Scruffy had worked at the slaughterhouse until a meat hook caught him in the eye. He now had an eye that looked like an overcooked poached egg. He was someone you didn't want to come across in the graveyard at night. That would really scare the crap out of you. Although he was harmless and didn't usually come out into public, especially during the day. He only had one friend in town and that was Robert Hall, the tramp. He got that name because he always wore all of his clothes on his back. He would have three coats, two shirts, and nobody knows how many pairs of pants on. Even in the summer on the hottest day of the year. They said he had more clothes than the men's store named "Robert Hall," hence his name "Robert Hall."

I didn't move a muscle, I just sat there hoping he would not see me. Luckily I was high up in the tree and he just walked on by. Then I heard a noise that sounded like an animal in trouble. It repeated the same sound over and over. I had seen enough animals in trouble this summer and did not want to see anymore. I was about to climb down from the tree when I saw Joe emerge from the woods. Again, I didn't move. I just hugged the tree and hoped he didn't see me or my bike.

Joe kept walking and never looked up. He had the horn that we had made slung over his back. That must have been the sound that I heard. I would remember what that sounded like, so I would know next time and start running in the opposite direction.

I waited up in the tree for about ten minutes to give Joe time to get out of sight. I didn't need any of the trouble that was sure to follow him.

I then climbed down and rode past Tubby's house to see if he was around. His father's truck was gone and I didn't see anyone, so I just kept pedaling and went home.

Nothing exciting happened the remainder of the summer. My mother was going to take me shopping for school clothes. I hated this more than going to the dentist's office. It also meant school would be starting soon, and I did not want to think about that. All those stupid classes like "penmanship," "ancient history," and "problems of democracy," I didn't need to know anything about that kind of stuff, and I knew how to write.

I could not wait for winter to arrive. I just wanted to go sled riding and skiing. That reminded me, I would have to get a pair of snowshoes. Maybe I could talk my mother into taking me to the Family Store while we were out shopping. They have all kinds of camping and sporting equipment on display. I like looking around in there even, if I don't buy anything.

Chapter 8

It was now September and Labor Day. That meant the county fair and school would be starting. I liked the fair, but I didn't like school. But it also meant that winter was not far away, and I couldn't wait for that.

I dreaded the first day of school. It always seemed as if I got the worst teachers. When I would tell my older friends who my teachers were they would always say, "Oh no, not her! She's a witch, you'll be sorry," or "That guy is the worst." It never failed, I always got the nastiest teachers.

I just hoped that Joe wasn't in any of my classes. So far I had been lucky and never had a class with him. He would get me into trouble somehow without even trying. I didn't need that; I could get into enough trouble without him.

I walked the mile and a half to school alone. I wasn't in the mood for company, I just wanted to get there and get it over with so I could get home and go up the hill and be in the cool woods. The school day was always the longest day, it took forever to be over. It seemed like it lasted much longer than seven hours.

First class was history, so boring, I didn't care what happened years ago. Second class was gym; that wasn't too bad. I liked climbing the ropes and doing stuff on the high bar and parallel bars that would be useful. Third class was penmanship. I hated this class, making all those circles and parallel lines with the old nib ink pen. That thing was like a weapon, it would be banned from schools nowadays. You could do some serious damage with one of those things. In fact, it did get me into trouble.

As luck would have it, Joe was in my penmanship class and he sat next to me. I tried to ignore him as much as possible, but it was hard. He kept talking to me and wanted me to put the pigtails of the girl sitting in front of me into the ink well. There was no way I was going to do that.

Our teacher was Miss Ball, also know as Paddle Happy Ball. She loved giving students a paddle. She had a special paddle with holes drilled into it to cut down on the air resistance so she cold get as much "ouch" out of the paddle as possible. I believe she also taught science and knew about this kind of stuff.

Since I would not dip the girl's pigtails into the ink well, Joe grabbed my pen and threw it as hard as he could into the wooden floor. It stuck in the wood, almost burying the entire point! Miss Ball was demonstrating how she wanted the parallel lines done on the chalkboard with her back turned to us. As soon as she heard the sound of the pen going into the floor, she turned around and saw me trying to pull it out of the floor.

"Daniel! Did you just throw your pen into the floor?" she screamed.

I couldn't squeal on Joe, it was an unwritten law that this just wasn't done. I had to think fast. "No, it just fell off of my desk as I was getting my tablet out," I answered.

"Don't you tell me that it just fell! I have been doing this longer than you have been on earth and I know the difference between a pen falling to the floor and one being thrown. Come out in the hall with me right now!" she yelled as she reached for the paddle hanging on the wall.

Oh no, not the paddle. This was no way to start the school year. I followed her out into the hall. I tried to explain that I did not throw the pen into the floor, but she would have none of it. "Bend over and hold on to the back of that chair."

I did as I was told and "whack, whack, whack." I lost count and just hoped it would soon end. It finally did. I returned to the classroom. All eyes were on me, except for Joe - he was looking out the window as if nothing happened.

I hoped my parents didn't find out about this, because it would be worse when I got home. I would get a good scolding and be grounded for a week. That would be much worse than the paddling I had received.

After class I confronted him, "Why did you do that?"

"I wanted to see if it would stick into the floor, that's all."

"Next time use your own pen, not mine."

"Did it hurt?"

"What do you think?" I replied as I turned and walked away from him. The next day I asked Miss Ball if I could sit up front so I could see the board better.

"I was going to move you up front anyway, so I could keep my eye on you. I can tell you are a trouble maker."

So started the school year. I could not wait for it to be over. I avoided Joe as much as I could that year, but even so, we did manage to get into more trouble. This was not going to be a good year.

It was a warm October Indian summer day, probably the last; at least I hoped it was the last. I couldn't wait for the snow to start falling. It was Saturday, and the leaves were turning colors. The hills were covered in red, yellow, and purple leaves. I was going to go up the hill and take a walk in the woods.

I stopped at Tubby's house to see if he wanted to come along. I called "Tuubby! Tubby!" from out on the street. My father would have had a fit if he knew that I did this.

Soon Tubby came out from around back, "What's up?" he asked.

"I'm going up to the woods. Want to come along?"

"It is a nice day, but I can't. My old man wants me to go with him to see Senator Kennedy, he's coming to Johnstown today. He thinks it would be a great experience for me, since he is going to be the next president of the United States."

"Your dad really thinks he is going to win?"

"Oh yeah, he said that Nixon is a real idiot and he will never be president. At least he hopes not."

"I'm not really interested in that kind of stuff, I just want to go to Ca...." I was cut off by Tubby before I could finish.

"I know...CANADA! You're never going to go to Canada."

"Oh, I'm going to go, you'll see." I then headed for the woods and left Tubby standing there. I don't know why everyone thought I would never go to Canada. I'd show them.

I entered the woods and was walking up the path when all of a sudden something came out of the bushes and jumped on me.

"Hey, Dandy! Where you headed?" screamed Joe. Great, the last person I wanted to see.

"I'm just going for a walk up in the woods. What are you doing? Going home I hope?"

"No, I just came from there. I was looking to see if I could find someone to go with me to watch JFK and his motorcade coming down Fairfield Avenue. Do you want to come?"

"I don't have any interest in that kind of stuff."

"You could tell everyone you saw the president of the United States if you came along. Then next week we could go and see Nixon. That way, no matter who wins, we could say we saw the president of the United States!"

"I would like to see the president of the United States. Not everyone can say that they have seen him. But I am only going down to Fairfield Avenue and then I'm coming back up here. I'm not going in to town to listen to a speech."

We both went back down the path past Tubby's house. His father's old truck was gone. They must have already left to go downtown.

When we got to Fairfield Avenue, there was a huge crowd on both sides of the street. The police on motorcycles were riding up and down the street to keep the spectators back and on the sidewalk.

There was still traffic moving up and down the street and a few people were starting to block the intersection at "J" Street. The police quickly arrived and made them move back onto the sidewalk. Little kids were riding their tricycles on the Beam School playground and the sidewalk leading up to the front door.

It was a carnival-like atmosphere; everyone was in a joyous mood. Housewives, who hadn't seen each other for a while, were catching up on the latest gossip. I was waiting for someone to come by selling hotdogs or peanuts.

Then a roar went up from the crowd on the corner above us and we could see police cars and motorcycles coming around the corner. Following them were a few cars and then a convertible came into view with someone sitting on the rear deck. We all assumed it was Kennedy.

The motorcade slowly made it's way down the street. Then Joe whispered in my ear, "When he comes by us, let's run up to his car and shake his hand!"

"Are you crazy?" I whispered back. I didn't want anyone to hear us either.

"Hey, we can say we shook the President's hand if he wins."

"The police won't let us out there," I told him.

"We'll see," whispered Joe.

The motorcade slowly made it's way toward us. Kennedy was waving at all the people and everyone was waving back and cheering.

The car was now only a few feet from us and Joe grabbed my arm and dragged me out into the road as the car approached us. To my surprise, when Kennedy saw us running toward him, he held out his had to shake our hands. Joe let go of my arm and shook JFK's hand and then I did the same.

When I turned around to run back to the sidewalk, I saw that everyone had followed us out into the street. Kennedy's car was being mobbed by the crowd. The police on motorcycles came rushing toward the car with their sirens blaring.

I knew this was the end of the line for Joe and me. We would probably spend the next few years in reform school for causing a riot. I was starting to tremble, and I didn't know what to do. But the police were more concerned about the crowd around the car than they were with us.

Joe and I both ran back to the sidewalk and back up the hill to our neighborhood. You could still hear the crowd cheering as the motorcade made it's way through town.

"Joe, you're crazy. We could have ended up in jail or reform school!"

"We didn't do anything wrong. We just shook his hand, that's all."

"There is never a dull moment when you are around, Joe."

"Things just happen to me, that's all. I bet you can't wait until Nixon comes to town. We are going to go see him."

"Not me! This was enough excitement."

Nixon did come to town a few weeks later, and as luck would have it, I ran into Joe that day. He did talk me into going to see Nixon, but just as we started down the brick road, it started to snow. We both had English bikes with skinny tires. The snow made the bricks slippery, like they were covered with grease. Both of us ended up sliding and falling off our bikes.

"That's it!" yelled Joe. "I'm not going anywhere but home in this weather. I can hardly stand up, let alone ride a bike. I'll see you tomorrow, Dandy."

I couldn't believe Joe gave up that easy. I was glad he did. I couldn't imagine what kind of trouble we would have gotten into if we had gone. Besides, I had to go home and wax my skis. Winter was finally here!

It was an early snow that year, but it only lasted a day or two. I did get to go sled riding and skiing though, and it was great. But Indian summer made an appearance and the snow melted.

On Sunday my dad would usually take us on a drive to various places if he wasn't working. This day we were going to look at the leaves. The fall colors were at their peak now. We drove out to the Rolling Rock Hunt Club and past all of the quaint stone houses that my father said reminded him of England. All of the houses had a pheasant plaque out on the fence with their name and box number.

We drove past one field that had a white section of fence and a hedge that the horses would jump over during their horse jumping rallies. Further along was a water hazard with flowers growing along the sides. It was a very picturesque scene surrounded by a split rail fence.

My father stopped the car and we got out and walked along the split rail fence. There were a few horses grazing in the field. As the cars drove by us on the road, the fallen leaves would appear to jump up and chase each car down the road. Then when they couldn't keep up the leaves would fall back down onto the pavement and wait for the next car to come by.

We went back to the car and then rode around in silence enjoying the views. Then we drove back out to the main highway and up over Laurel Mountain past the ski slope and down the other side. We stopped at the Twin Lakes Store and walked around the two small ponds in back. There were ducks and Canadian geese swimming around on the ponds. From up here you could look down over the valleys and see all of the countryside aglow in crimson and golden yellow colors.

We went over to the tables they had set up with corn stalks, Indian corn, and apple cider. My father bought a gallon of cider.

This cider was very sweet. Cider had a different taste at each place that sold it.

Then we ended up in Vinco, outside of Johnstown, and we stopped at The Emerald Ice Cream shop that I always enjoyed. Not so much for the ice cream, although I did like it, but for the monkeys they had in the backroom. I never did figure out how monkeys ended up in an ice cream shop. They were in a large cage with swings hanging from the top, and perches on the sides where they would sit and look at the people and hold out their hands for treats that were sold in machines.

After receiving a treat they would drop it in their mouth and start clamoring for more. Then they would dangle from the swings and swing back and forth from swing to swing. The whole time they were making monkey noises. After a while it became unbearable and we went outside and sat at one of the picnic tables under the large oak trees. It was a beautiful Indian summer day.

October was a spooky time of the year. It had been raining all week and every time I went outside I had to take an umbrella with me. I was going out; I could not stand being in the house for another minute. I am an outdoor person. I got a job delivering the morning newspaper, and I had to get up at 4:30 am every day except Sunday. They did not have a Sunday paper back then. As I was going out the door I grabbed an umbrella from the old milk can, where we kept them, and I opened it up.

All of a sudden I heard my mother screaming, "Dandy! What on earth do you think you are doing? You know better than to open an umbrella in the house! We are all going to have bad luck for the next year now."

"Oh, Mom, that is just a superstition. Nothing is going to happen."

"Just wait and see. You'll be sorry you did that. Don't ever do it again, I'm warning you!"

"Ok, I won't," she would have been shocked to know that I had walked under ladders, kept walking straight when a black cat crossed in front of me, and I even broke a mirror once.

"Where do you think you are going anyway? It is pouring down rain outside."

"I am going to the little store to see what costume I can come up with for Halloween."

"Oh, go ahead and go, but come straight home!"

"I will."

The next morning I got up at 4:30 am and, as usual, my mother had my bowl of cereal waiting for me.

"You know what today is, don't you?" She didn't wait for an answer. "It's Friday the 13th, and after that stunt you pulled last night, you better be very careful."

"Mom, that is just a superstition. Nothing is going to happen today or any day, you wait and see."

"Boy, for your sake I hope you are right."

I left the house and went down to pick up my first batch of 99 papers. After I delivered those, I had to stop at another pick-up spot, where there were 50 more. I put the papers in my sack and started folding them so I could throw them on to the porches. Otherwise, I would place them between the storm door and door, or wedge them between the doorknob and jam if there was no storm door.

Then there were the easy ones, the apartment buildings. All I had to do was go inside and just drop the newspaper that was folded in half in front of their door. I liked doing these; some apartment buildings had five or six customers in each one. That was how it was at Building 13 on 13th Street. The apartments were above the drug store. I never gave it much thought before, but as I entered the building I started counting the steps up to the second floor... 13 steps! I was thinking how my mother would react to this. Here it is Friday the 13th, and I am entering building 13 on 13th Street, walking up 13 steps to the second floor. She would have a fit!

I had done this several hundred times and never gave it any thought. I am sure I had done this at least once or twice on a Friday the 13th. My mother's words kept popping into my head, "You better be very careful."

Superstition, that's all it was. Nothing is going to happen. I delivered all the papers and walked down the steps and counted them again, just to make sure I didn't miscount. Nope, 13 steps; the same as before. I opened the door to go out and just as I was about to step out, I noticed everything had changed. There were no tall brick buildings; they were all one or two story wooden structures. The big marble-covered bank on the corner was gone. The road was dirt and the sidewalks were made of wooden planks.

I jumped back into the building and slammed the door shut. I ran up the steps and looked around. The papers were still there, and everything appeared normal. I was hoping someone would come out of their apartment and go to work, but no one did. I didn't know what to do. This was the only apartment building that didn't have any windows, not even on the door.

I walked back down the 13 steps to the door. I slowly turned the knob. When it wouldn't turn any further, I gradually opened the door and peeked out of the widening crack. I saw the road was paved and the sidewalks were cement. I saw the big marble-covered bank on the corner. Everything appeared normal.

I cautiously stepped onto the sidewalk while holding on to the door jam, just incase everything changed. It didn't, and I went on my way and completed my route without any other problems.

I have often wondered what would have happened if I had stepped out into the past on that fateful day. Would I have gone back in time? Would I have had to stay there?

I never told Tubby or anyone else about what happened that day. I was sure they would think I was crazy. I learned my lesson that day! Don't open an umbrella indoors and be very careful on Friday the 13th!

The Soviet Union had launched the Sputnik satellite a couple of years previously and the US was launching rockets and trying to catch up. Everyone was saying that is why we had such hot summers and bad winters. "Those rockets and satellites are messing the weather up," they would say. My grandfather told me that is what the cavemen said when the bow and arrow was invented. "Those newfangled bows and arrows are messing up the weather!"

That year they launched Echo. It took about 90 minutes to circle the earth and it went over Johnstown on its orbit. The newspaper would publish the time it would go over on the back page.

Tubby and I would always watch it go over. It would come up in the west and go right overhead and fade away in the east.

Halloween was only a day away and we had just turned the clocks back and it was getting dark an hour earlier and there were times when we could see Echo go over twice.

We checked the time in the newspaper, 8:20 pm, it read. It was only after 7:00 and it was already dark. We went out in my backyard to wait for it to come over. There were too many trees in Tubby's yard, and I only had one small chestnut tree in my yard and a great view of the sky.

It was a very cool, clear night and we both had coats and hats on. The moon was not full yet and there were millions of stars in the sky. We had a great view.

"It won't be coming for another hour or more," said Tubby.

"I know," I replied. "Maybe we will see some shooting stars while we wait."

"OK, you look east and I will look west."

We laid down on the damp grass and looked up at the sky.

"If you see any, holler out because they go fast," I told him.

"I will, don't worry."

After about ten minutes Tubby yelled, "Here comes Echo!"

"It can't be, it's too early."

Tubby looked at his Hopalong Cassidy watch, "It's an hour early. I bet the paper forgot to adjust for daylight savings time, that is why it is an hour off."

We watched the light coming across the sky. It seemed brighter tonight. I assumed because it was such a clear and cool night with no humidity that it could be seen clearer. It traveled the usual path and was coming directly overhead. That was when we both heard the low hum coming from the light.

Echo never made a sound when it went over, but tonight there was a noise similar to the dial tone on a telephone. We both looked at each other.

"I don't think that was Echo," whispered Tubby.

"I don't think so, either. It seemed brighter than usual, and did you hear that noise it made?" I asked him. "It didn't sound like an airplane or a jet."

90

"Oh yeah, I heard it alright. Echo is just a big balloon, it does not make any noise."

"Then what did we just see?"

"I guess it was a flying saucer. It looked just like Echo, a bright steady light, but it made a noise. I don't know what else it could have been, do you?"

"I don't think it was Echo, I know that. Maybe the time in the paper is correct, then. Let's see if Echo does come at 8:20."

"My old man said there were flying saucers flying around the White House a few years ago, maybe they have come back."

"Do you think they came from Mars?" I asked him.

"I don't know where they came from. My old man doesn't know, either."

"You mean to tell me that there are some things your father doesn't know?"

"Ha, ha. Very funny, Dandy. He did say that people from outer space have already been here. If you have blue or green eyes, or blonde or red hair, then you are descended from the space people."

"What?? You mean because I have blue eyes, I'm from outer space? That's crazy!"

"I didn't say YOU were from outer space, I said you were descended from someone from outer space. And, I have blonde hair."

With that we patiently waited, both of us looking toward the western sky, hoping to see Echo. That would mean we really did see a flying saucer; otherwise, Echo has started making a noise.

"There it is!" yelled Tubby. Sure enough, at 8:20 Echo appeared in the west. Not quite as bright as the previous light we had seen, and there was a slight wobble to its path that I did not notice with the first light that went over.

It was now directly overhead and there was no hum, no noise at all. It was silent and wobbled away.

"I didn't hear anything that time, did you, Dandy?"

"No, there was no noise at all and it wasn't as bright at the first one that went over," I told him.

"Yeah, I noticed that, too, and it sort of wobbled."

"We have seen a flying saucer!"

The next night we couldn't wait to go out and watch for Echo. We repeated what we did the night before and we lay on the grass, one of us looking east and the other west. This time Tubby had brought a pair of binoculars.

Only a few minutes passed when I yelled, "Tubby! Here it comes from the wrong direction!"

I was pointing at a bright light in the east. Again, the light was brighter than Echo, moving about the same speed. It was a steady light, no blinking lights like an airplane would have. As it got overhead, we could hear the humming noise coming from the light.

When Tubby looked at it through the binoculars, he told me he could see that it was not saucer shaped but triangular with several rows of white lights across the bottom that started out with one light in the narrow end and increased in number as it got to the wider end.

He gave me the binoculars and I could see that he was correct in his description of the object. I had never seen anything like this, not even in comic books.

It kept going with no wobble and faded off in the west. We both looked at each other in disbelief. What had we just seen? Who should we tell? People would think we were either making it up or we were crazy. We couldn't tell anyone.

We didn't say much to each other, there was nothing we could say. We just sat there in silence knowing that Echo would soon be coming out of the west. Unless the flying saucer took it or crashed into it, they appeared to be in the same orbit.

About a half an hour later we saw Echo coming out of the west. Not quite as bright with a slight wobble and no noise when it went overhead.

We kept looking for our flying saucer that year and the following years, but we didn't see it. We did see many shooting stars and some with long tails like comets, but not our humming flying saucer.

A few weeks later I had got up enough courage to tell Joe what we had seen that October night, and of course he had a story to top it.

"Is that all you saw?" he asked me. "It was probably just a new type of jet the air force is working on. I once saw a long light like a fluorescent tube tumble across the sky. Now that's what I call a flying saucer!"

Chapter 9

Halloween had come and gone and the weather had turned colder. The leaves had fallen and the trees were mere skeletons now. All the surrounding hillsides were a bleak gray and I couldn't wait for the snow to arrive and brighten everything up.

The snow would cover everything in a thick white blanket and hide all the unsightliness. It was the most beautiful time of the year. I would go up the hill and look over at the gas line high up on the next hill. It was much higher and the snow would always lay there first. When I saw snow there, I knew it would not be long until there would be snow on our hill. I would spend my time waxing my skis and thinking about skiing or sled riding. I couldn't wait. Winter was my middle name!

Tubby and I had set up a trap line. This would be useful when I went to Canada. I could eat the meat and sell the furs. We had bought two traps each. They were size 1 Victor jaw traps. They had a chain and a ring on them to fasten them to a stake.

We would go out every day after school and check the traps. We had been doing this for a few weeks and had no luck so far. I thought it would be cool to trap a fur-bearing animal and tan its hide. I would buy *Field and Stream* magazine and look at the ads. There were ads for hunting and trapping equipment, and want-ads for furs. I had visions of selling my furs and making enough money to pay for my move to Canada.

Then one Saturday morning, when Tubby and I were checking the trap line, we saw that I had trapped a rabbit in my trap.

"Look, Dandy! You got a rabbit," yelled Tubby.

"He's still alive!" I screamed.

"Of course he is. The trap just closes on his leg when it goes off. Foxes have been known to chew off their leg to get out of the trap."

"Now what am I supposed to do?" I asked him.

"Get a club and hit him over the head, then gut him."

"There is NO way I am going to do that," I told him. I went over and released the jaws of the trap and the rabbit ran off.

"Why did you do that?"

"I can't kill any animals like that. If that is how you trap, then I am finished with it."

"What are you going to do when you go to Canada? You will have to live off of fish for the rest of your life!"

"Then that's what I will do. But I am not going to trap, that's for sure."

That ended it for me. No more trapping. I gathered up my traps and headed home. I would have to find a different way to make a living when I went to Canada.

It was Thanksgiving and it was a cold gray day. The clouds were getting thicker and darker. I was on my bike riding around the neighborhood. No one else was around. The puddles all had a thin cover of ice that would break like glass as I rode over them.

Then it started to snow - just flurries, but it was a start. Soon the ground was covered with a light coat of snow. The gray landscape was now looking brighter as the snow piled up on everything. I couldn't wait to get home and put another coat of wax on my skis. I would even put wax on my sled runners to make it go faster down the hills. Winter was finally here!

It snowed all that evening. Not a storm, but enough for a few inches to pile up by the next morning. I got up and looked over at the graveyard. It was all white and just waiting for me to start sled riding. It wasn't deep enough for skiing, but sled riding was just as much fun.

After breakfast I grabbed my sled and ran as fast as I could to the graveyard. No one was there yet. I had the whole place to myself. It seemed like only a short time until other kids showed up with their sleds and snow saucers. Andy came with a huge wooden toboggan that could seat at least five. Then Tubby came with his Duralite sled.

"I guess your dad is working today," I told him.

"Yeah, otherwise I would have brought my skis or gone to the dump to get a refrigerator door. But the snow isn't deep enough for that yet," he told me.

We spent the rest of the day sled riding down the hill and walking back up. Then Tubby looked at his watch and said, "I have to go, my old man will be home soon. He'll throw a fit if he sees that I had this sled out. See you tomorrow, Dandy."

"Ok, maybe it will snow tonight and we can get our skis out." I then noticed that I was the only one left there. Good, now I had the whole place to myself. I spent the remainder of the day going down that hill and walking back up. Winter! Life was good!

Then I heard my mother calling me. Oh, oh, it must be suppertime! I can't be late for that. I hoped my father wasn't home yet. I don't want to be late. I took off running, pulling my sled behind me.

"Your father will be home any minute. You just made it. You know how he gets when you're late for supper," she told me.

"It must be my lucky day," I replied. "It snowed enough to go sled ridding and I'm not late for supper."

Soon it would be Christmas, the best time of the year. Everyone was always in a good mood and winter would be here to stay. I couldn't wait. The snow had been piling up the last few weeks and it was going to be a white Christmas. I went skiing or sled riding every day after school and on the weekends.

It was Christmas Eve. The excitement was building. I couldn't wait until Christmas morning. My mother could see how anxious I was. She said we didn't get a wreath for the door and told me to go out to the woods and bring back a bag of Princess Pine. It was a funny looking green plant that only grew in moist areas in the woods. It would take a while to get a bag full.

I went up the hill and after a few hours I had the bag filled to the top. I ran home and got an old coat hanger and made it into a circle with the hooked part at the top. I then started wrapping the Princess Pine around the coat hanger and tied it on with thin wire. It didn't look half bad, even if I must say so myself.

It was almost 7:00. It would be time for "Almahl and the Night Visitors" to come on the television. It was an opera and I was not really fond of opera, but it had become a tradition watching it on Christmas Eve. I looked in the paper to see what channel it was on and it wasn't listed!

"Mom!! What happened to Almahl?" I asked her.

96

"They are not putting it on TV anymore. They are showing "A Christmas Carol" instead. You will like that."

What? Not more singing! I didn't want to watch a bunch of people singing Christmas carols. It wouldn't seem like Christmas without Almahl. We could only get two stations, and the other station had a Flash Gordon movie. That was not very Christmas-like.

I decided to check out "A Christmas Carol." I turned on the TV; of course we only had black and white. Color TVs had been invented, but my father said there were only a few programs that were in color and it wasn't worth the price of a color TV.

The movie started out with people singing carols in the street - not quite what I had expected. Then it got better. This guy named Scrooge was sure a mean one and ghosts were haunting him! I am glad I watched it. I would have to remember to watch it again next year.

The evening finally ended and I went to bed. I had a hard time falling asleep. I could see the snow falling under the streetlight. That made me feel good. I didn't know what I was getting for Christmas, probably clothes. I would have to wait and see.

Morning finally came. I ran out into the living room and there were many presents under the tree. I looked to see if there were any strange looking packages, but there was nothing unusual. I sat there waiting for my parents to get up. After what seemed like and eternity, they finally came into the living room.

"I'll put the kettle on for tea," my mother said to my father.

"Right O! I could go for a hot cuppa!" my father yelled out to her.

Now I had to wait for my mother to come back. The suspense was killing me. She finally came back into the room. We each took a turn opening our presents. The first two I had opened were clothes, pants and a shirt. It was not looking good. Then I opened the big square present. It felt heavy, not like an article of clothing.

It was a pair of felt lined winter boots. Just what I needed. Now my feet wouldn't get so cold. The next, and last, one, was the smallest and I thought since it was so small it probably wasn't anything very good.

I opened it up and it was a stainless steel hand warmer in a red carrying bag. Wow, now my hands won't get cold, either. The way the snow was coming down, I was going to need these very soon. This was one of the best Christmases ever!

After breakfast I put on my new boots, fired up my hand warmer, grabbed my sled, and headed for the graveyard. As usual I was the first one there. I was starting to believe that no one else really liked winter the way that I did. I couldn't believe it. Everyone had to like winter, it was the best time of the year!

Soon a few kids showed up with their new sleds or snow saucers, and one kid came with what looked like a ski on a frame similar to a bicycle. What's with that? I had never seen anything like it. Someone else brought a toboggan; not as big as Andy's, only big enough for two.

It didn't take long for the place to get crowded. After sledding down the hill I had to be careful walking back up. Those kids on the snow saucers would come flying down the hill and they could not control them. If one weren't careful, they would get run over.

I spent the whole Christmas vacation sled riding and skiing, and my hands and feet never got cold. But all good things must come to an end. It was New Year's Day before I knew it. I would have to go back to school. I couldn't bear to think about it. By the time I got home, my mother would have the tree down and it would be sitting out in the front yard. It wouldn't be there long. The Orthodox Christmas was only a week away. One of them would come and take the tree and put it up in their house.

This was the saddest day of the year. Christmas was over, school had started again. The only good thing was that winter was just starting and every day after school and every weekend I would be skiing or sled riding. No better time than winter! Winter is my middle name!!

Chapter 10

As I sit here watching my wife undecorate the Christmas tree, I think back about those Christmases long ago. I never did go to Canada - Tubby was right after all. Although, I did go there on vacation with my parents. We went to Niagara Falls and the Welland Canal. But it was so flat there, I couldn't see any place where one could go sled riding or skiing. Any way, I didn't like the idea of trapping. I couldn't kill those animals.

I did get a job at the "Tic-Toc" restaurant as a dishwasher and potato peeler. That was not a job I wanted to make into a career. I had to bleach the cups every other Tuesday and clean the deep fryers on the other Tuesday. I would come home smelling like bleach and potatoes.

Tubby went to collage to become a teacher. I couldn't believe it when he told me what he was going to do.

"How could you spend the rest of your life in school??" I asked him.

"What, do you think I am going to be a dishwasher like you?" he told me.

"I'm not going to be a dishwasher forever. I have put in my application at Glosser Brothers. Then I can work my way up and be a manager someday."

"Yeah, just like you are going to go to Canada."

He became a teacher and moved to a town about two hours away and I haven't seen or heard from him in over 40 years.

I did get a job at Glosser Brothers department store as a clerk/stock boy. I made minimum wage - $1.15 an hour. The manager of the men's department told me "If you do a good job, I will make you an assistant manager like Sam over there."

I asked Sam how much he made an hour and he whispered, "I make $1.25 an hour!"

I knew then that I was not going to make this a career, either. That was only ten cents more than I was earning. Two weeks later I got hired at Bethlehem Steel Company, making a whopping

$2.25 an hour! I was rich! Living at home, I had more money than I could spend. I saved as much as possible, got married, and we built our own house. Working with my grandfather had paid off.

I even worked in the Coke Plant, and it was just a disgusting as Deadeye had described it! It was the dirtiest place I that I ever worked. The first two weeks I worked there, I could not eat my lunch - the smell there was unbearable. But after that I got used to it. Luckily, I only had to work there a few months. I worked in the Axle Plant and then ended up in steel making.

Joe never joined the carnival. Like me, of course, he went to work in the steel mill. It seems as though I was doomed to have Joe following me everywhere I went! He became a plant grievance man, one of the best that there was, at least that was what he said.

"Hey, Joe, I have a grievance," I told him.

"Oh yeah? What is it?" he asked me.

"Well this past winter I moved up to forklift operator, hauling axles outside for storage, and I almost froze to death. The forklifts don't have a roof and there are no heaters on them. Every fifteen minutes I had to stop and get warm."

"Yeah, but you like the winter, if I remember correctly."

"I do, but my beef is that when summer came this guy that has more time than me bumped me off my job and I had to go inside as the axle checker in forge. Those axles are 1800 degrees when they come out of the hammers and it is 90 degrees out. My point is he can't just move from a nice warm job in the winter then take my cool job now that summer is here. Now I have a hot job in the summer and a cold job in the winter. This is not right and I want you to do something about it!"

"Dandy, this is 'past practice' and there is nothing you can do about it."

"What do you mean 'past practice'?"

"They have been doing this so long now, that it is past practice."

"That's a bunch of crap, Joe!" I screamed at him. "I'm sorry, Joe. I didn't mean to yell. This is the eighth day in a row that I have been working."

100

"Just think of all the extra money you have made," he said trying to make me feel better.

"What do you mean, 'extra money'? I worked the last five days of last week and the first three this week; I didn't work more than five days in one week, so I didn't get paid time and half for anything."

"Well, you have a grievance there. If you work more than five days in a row over a two week period, you get paid time and half for the sixth and seventh consecutive days. I will help you file for that."

"Good, at least you helped me with something. But that 'past practice' stuff is a bunch of crap!"

Over the years Joe did help me file a few grievances, and we got along a lot better after that. I do still see Joe occasionally while shopping or out on the street. We don't hang out together, though.

Andy told me was going to go to college and study political science. "You're going to be what kind of scientist?" I asked him.

"I'm not going to be a scientist, I am going to study political science. You know, be a politician," he explained.

"Why on earth would you want to be a politician?"

"You can't beat that job, Dandy. They have more time off than any other profession, even teachers. They are always on some kind of a break. Besides, I can go on junkets to the Alps or Colorado and go skiing there. You know how much I like to ski."

"You have a point there. Well, good luck and don't forget about us little people."

He did get involved in politics and eventually moved to Washington DC. He came home a few times at first, asking everyone to vote for him. Then he lost an election and I never saw him again. Someone said they heard he moved to Colorado and was working at a ski slope there. It is ironic that Joe and I were the only ones that talked about leaving Johnstown and it ended up that we were the only two that stayed here.

This has been the warmest winter I have ever known. I don't remember a winter where we only had snow on the ground for three or four days. That is how it has been this winter. At least I don't have to shovel the 100-foot driveway! Although, I do have a snow blower now.

After I got married we built a house overlooking the pond at the old Clackum farm. It looks more like a lodge than a house with all of the wood on the inside. A large fireplace in the living room and a wood burner down in the family room. It is just how I imagined the cabin along the lake in Canada would look, only my house is much bigger than the cabin would have been.

I can look out the windows and see kids ice skating on the pond and sled riding down through the fields. We have even gone cross-country skiing there, but now we mainly go snow shoeing. We don't want to break any bones.

I still check the sky for flying saucers, and 25 years after that October day, when Tubby and I saw that object, I saw it travel over our house. It was a steady light and hummed when overhead. I had my binoculars and I saw that it was triangular with several rows of lights across the underside, just like the first time. But I don't think it was a flying saucer or a UFO as they are now called but I believe it was something our government was testing, like the Stealth. Although, it is hard to believe that they had the Stealth in 1960!

Now we have the space station, communication and spy satellites, and who knows what orbiting the earth. They have since discovered earth-like planets only four light years away. Who knows what is up there.

Times have changed since Tubby, Joe, and I were kids. Now everyone has a cell phone. If there had been cell phones when we were growing up, we would not have had some of our adventures. The Gypsy would not have needed us to carry a note, she would have just made a phone call.

I do miss the simpler times. Now everyone walks down the street with ear buds in their ears or they seem to be talking to themselves. If we had seen someone walking along with their hand up to their ear talking away, we would have thought they were crazy and knew they would end up in the loony bin.

Well I have to go put the boxes of Christmas decorations up in the attic. I do hate to see the Christmas tree coming down. It is a very sad day. Oh well, just 350 more days and I will be going back up into the attic to bring these boxes back down. Happy New Year to everyone!! I hope it is a good year for you. It just started snowing and the snowflakes are as big as half dollars. Winter is my middle name. It is going to be a good year!

THE END

****

Thank you for your support. Could you please leave a review on AMAZON when you are finished reading this book? Thank You!
Don Rayner

32964497R00068

Made in the USA
Lexington, KY
07 March 2019